Apradhini

Apradhini

Women without Men

Shivani

Translated from the Hindi

by Ira Pande

HARPERPERENNIAL

An Imprint of HarperCollins *Publishers*

HARPERPERENNIAL

First published in India by Harper Perennial 2010
An imprint of HarperCollins *Publishers*
4th Floor, Tower A, Building No. 10, DLF Cyber City,
DLF Phase II, Gurugram, Haryana – 122002
www.harpercollins.co.in

This edition published in India by Harper Perennial 2024

2 4 6 8 10 9 7 5 3 1

P-ISBN: 978-93-5699-731-8
E-ISBN: 978-93-5116-067-0

Typeset in 11/15 Goudy Old Style at
SŪRYA

Printed and bound at
Thomson Press (India) Ltd.

MIX
Paper from
responsible sources
FSC® C010615

This book is produced from independently certified FSC® paper
to ensure responsible forest management.

Contents

Translator's Acknowledgements

I would like to thank my siblings, Veena, Mrinal and Muktesh, for allowing me to access the Hindi texts for this book and for the warm support they have provided all through.

Thanks also to my son Aditya for the 2010 edition's cover design and to the team at HarperCollins India, Karthika, Pradipta and Shuka, for their help and suggestions.

The story 'Alakh Mai' was first published in my book, *Diddi: My Mother's Voice*, Penguin India, 2005. I am grateful for their permission to use it here.

Prologue

I never write a preface or epilogue to any story or novel. Like Virginia Woolf, I believe that a preface to a book is like a piece of cardboard that is used to steady a shaky table. If a table has shaky legs, it has no right to exist. A work of writing should be strong enough to stand on its own, without the help of a cardboard support, declares Woolf. One day, when the piece of cardboard is removed, the table will become unsteady once again.

However, today I am breaking a self-imposed rule because I think my pen wants me to do so. Almost every day, I get hundreds of letters from my readers asking me questions such as: why did you write this, what inspired you, is this story true? Sometimes, I feel as if I am a fish in an aquarium, whose every move is observed. Writing gives me immense pleasure, but talking of my characters – their joys and sorrows, their fears and desires – is very difficult. This is because I often feel I have not been able to fully bring out what I had in mind. Janaki's intoxicating gaze, which

I could see so clearly, refused to be translated when I sat down to describe it. I discarded countless sheets of paper, but still the expression in her eyes remained elusive. It was as if she moved just before my camera had been able to click, or my film had got exposed. The fleshy lips of Muggi, or the gold glinting in the teeth of the warden's grin – have I been able to portray these as I wished to?

This is the frustration a writer is often confronted with – I saw, heard and experienced the pain of these characters in an environment that is impossible to convey in words and images. And what experiences they were! Among them was the pathetic request of a Kumaoni girl, whose story absorbed me so completely that I forgot where I was. For a brief moment, both of us became oblivious to the hot loo that raged outside and were transported from the cell to a land where cool breezes blow down mountainsides. It is one of the ironies of life that we are unable to accept the truth unless we can see, feel or hear it. And yet, whether we accept it or not, nothing can ever change the truth. However, there is another kind of truth: the sort that we accept simply because it is there. For a brief moment, I was back with Chanuli in her village, and it was the hour when the cows come home – what we call '*godhuli*' in Hindi. The prison, its walls and the searing afternoon heat – all vanished before the truth of Chanuli's story.

A prison can also make a writer's imagination oddly redundant. The characters I met there converted me into a sort of medium – a planchette if you wish – and my pen wrote down whatever stories were revealed to me.

Unfortunately, I cannot write of those whose cases are still sub judice, yet there are some faces that will forever haunt me. A fourteen-year-old girl whose eyes welled up at the sound of a kind voice – what crime could she have committed to barter away her whole life? She had been persuaded by her seventy-year-old uncle to get her young lover to the house; the old man implicated her in the murder he committed and left her to her fate when he died. Along with her was a woman whom everyone called 'Maa-ji'. Her tall and upright bearing was topped with a face that had the slyest eyes I've ever seen. Even in the prison, she had managed to collect a band of devotees and her voice, when it rang out, vaulted over the prison walls in thrilling cascades. Her hooded eyes contained dark secrets that I cannot reveal until her case has been decided by the courts. Embezzlement, fraud, cheating gullible villagers – she was guilty on all these counts. My fingers itch to write about the countless characters I encountered there, but the laws of the court forbid me to do so.

Kalhan writes in the *Rajatarangini* that a writer should be able to uncover emotional diseases the way a surgeon's knife lances tumours. What else can prove that he has the gift of healing? But this is easier said than done. When *Dharmayug* was serializing *Ja Re Ekaki*, I was flooded with protests from the government. How dare I write that the children in the prison school were unhappy, or of their pale faces? Did I know that they were given milk every day? I did not see the need to justify what I had written, but I will tell them now that there are some environments where no life can prosper or thrive. Even if those children were given the best milk the government could procure, I can wager that their pale faces would never bloom healthily.

Some months after my visit to the women's prison, I received an invitation from another one. This time, I was invited to visit on raksha bandhan and tie rakhis on some male prisoners' wrists. Usually, I avoid these empty gestures made by well-meaning social organizations. This one-day charity is not my cup of tea at all. Moreover, when I often forget my own brothers on rakhi, how could I take on the responsibility of acquiring some more? But this time, I felt compelled to go.

When I entered the vast hall and was confronted with rows of prisoners seated neatly, my heart sank. I remembered hearing in my childhood that all murderers are issued a special uniform to distinguish them from the others when I saw five men, clad in identical yellow clothes, come towards me. They had been chosen as the representatives of the whole body of inmates and were the ones on whose wrists I would tie the sacred thread. Each one them, chosen today for exemplary behaviour in the prison, was guilty of killing another human being. My new brothers approached me and, when they knelt in front of me, their wrists spread obediently in my direction, they seemed to me like the actors from a Ramlila who had put on the masks of a demon for the duration of the play and had now unmasked themselves to mark the end of a performance. Their clean faces, shining with a palpable affection and devotion, bore no trace of the hideous roles they had played earlier. Truly, they appeared no different from any brother.

'This is Singh' – the warden introduced the first one with a smile. 'He recites wonderful verses. And this one' – he introduced the next prisoner – 'is a marvellous singer. His band is famous even outside the prison.' The poet bent low over my feet: tall and handsome, he could well have been a hero in one of my novels. I remembered the lines of the Bengali poet Kashiram I had read years ago:

Dekho dvija mansij
jinya murati
Khagraj paay laaj
nasika atul

Look at the twin Kamadevas,
the handsome lords of love –
their aquiline nose puts to shame
even the grand Garuda

The ceremony over, drums and cymbals struck a lively tune as they sang:

Yeh hai ujde watan ka chaman bhaiyyo
bahene ayi to isme bahar aa gayi

This is otherwise a wilderness, my brothers,
but spring has followed our sisters here today

I could follow the sweet voice of my new brother throughout: just as there is a young qawwal whose clear soprano rings high over the deeper notes of the rest of the singers, his voice soared over that of the rest like a nightingale's. Those of you who have heard the high-pitched voice of Master Madan will understand what I mean. This man was the music director of the prison and brilliant at his job. Then, one day, I am told, he made an unusual request: could he take his band outside the prison to play at weddings or parties? Naturally, he was turned down – who could allow such dangerous players to step outside a prison? Suppose they snatched a rifle from an enthusiastic man accompanying a wedding procession – what could they not do with it? 'I beg you, sir,' he had pleaded, 'just give me one chance. I promise you I will not let you down.' Miraculously, he succeeded in convincing the staff and he was true to his word. Now, I was told, he was in great demand all over the town; and what is more, never once has he cheated on his promise to return to the prison at the appointed hour.

My glance ran over the faces in front of me, trying to see beyond the polite masks, and my eyes picked out one whose face was buried in his knees. Throughout the ceremony, he did not lift it even once. All I could make out from his slender shoulders was that he was very young and my imagination began to spin tales. I listened with half my mind on him to the poems being recited and the songs being sung, and my hands clapped mechanically – I simply could not take my eyes off those defeated shoulders. I was tempted to ask the warden who the young boy was, but I could not get myself to intrude into a grief so private. Obviously, he wanted to have nothing to do with the world, he had ducked out of sight – what right had I to disturb his retreat?

Finally, I turned to the warden. 'There must be some children from the juvenile home here today – why don't I tie a rakhi on the youngest member from there?' Within a few minutes, the young boy stood before me, his wrist outstretched obediently. I held his wrist; it was burning with fever. I was told he had insisted on coming and specially worn his NCC uniform for the occasion. I tied the simple silk thread on his wrist, regretting that I did not have the kind of flashy rakhi that my young son ordered: one with a plastic aeroplane or a watch studded on gaudy tinsel. Poor little boy, I thought, what crime could he have possibly committed? My feelings must have reflected on my face, for the warden smiled as he said: 'This is a very brave boy, aren't you, son? Last year, he shot a friend with his father's gun.'

This boy? He had shot someone dead?

They had been playing a game of marbles, and an argument had ballooned into a full-fledged fight. The boy ran inside, picked up his father's loaded rifle and shot his friend dead. The impact of the shot felled him as well and both friends lay side by side. Except that one of them was dead. He was sentenced to three years in a remand home and sent to the juvenile home.

He was followed by a Muslim boy, who was serving the last year of his sentence. He must have been only fifteen or sixteen, for his upper lip had a faint trace of down and his voice was still breaking. By now, I had no curiosity left – whatever the crime, the punishment seemed far in excess of it.

'What class are you in?' I asked him.

'Ninth,' he replied, head low.

'Where is your home?'

'Ji, in Rampura.'

His lips were trembling, perhaps in dread of the question he thought I would ask next: why are you here? Of course, I did not. He turned away swiftly and was soon lost in the crowd.

'Do you know how important these rakhis are for the men you have tied them on?' the warden asked me later. 'They put them in their Ramayana or holy book and look upon them as their sisters.'

I felt as if I would choke. Who knows whether my rakhis were pressed between the pages of a Ramayana or a Koran – and I realized then that, whether or not I had a rakhi pressed in the pages of my books, I would never forget the faces of these brothers. That bent head, the sweet soprano, the shy poet – they stand eternally before me.

I know that mere stories do not engage readers for long; until they can sense the writer's own emotions behind a character, stories remain dull and lifeless to readers. I do not know how far I have succeeded in bringing alive these characters, but when these stories were being serialized in *Dharmayug* and *Saptahik Hindustan*, I was drowned in fan mail. Someone had recognized a character from an incident she had witnessed in Tikamgarh thirty years ago.

'That maalin is from Tikamgarh, isn't she?' she wrote. 'When the police were taking her, the crowd passed in front of our house. I still remember her face and the gunny bag that contained the remains of the husband she had murdered.'

Yes, she was the same maalin. On the pretext of taking her ailing husband to the toilet, she had led him to her lover's hatchet. Then the two had dug a pit and buried him nearby. A few days later, a huge downpour had uncovered their hideous crime and the dead man's hand had risen from the earth as if in accusation. Another reader recognized Janaki, another character I had written about.

'If you could write about her,' she wrote to me, 'then would you like to hear my story?'

I tore up the letter. I am no voyeur, I wanted to tell her. I don't write to titillate.

As I recall the faces I saw in my visits to the prison, I am reminded of Habib Tanvir's brilliant play, *Agra Bazaar*. I hear the three fakirs, clad in their flowing, tattered robes, tambourine in hand, coming towards me from behind the wings of a stage. I cannot see them yet, but their sweet voices echo all around the hall:

Gul shor babula aag hava
Aur keechar pani mitti hai
Hum dekh chuke is duniya ko
Yeh dhoke ki si tatti hai . . .

A ball of fire, a gust of hot wind
Mud, water and slime
We have seen this world, my friends
It is a mirage, a false curtain . . .

PART ONE

Chanuli

Just before Holi, sometime in March or so, the postman brought me two invitations.

One was from a prosperous Ladies Club: set in acres of green, velvety lawns, it had lines of posh cars outside it when I reached. An unending stream of beautifully dressed women in their kotas, chanderis and mulmuls were alighting, leaving trails of perfume behind them. The occasion was a pre-Holi celebration and the ladies had invited a well-known qawwal to sing the traditional Horis. Rose-water was sprinkled on the guests and clouds of abeer-gulal coloured the atmosphere. Tinkling laughter greeted me as I walked in and uniformed waiters with trays of drinks and snacks circulated discreetly among the guests. I was proudly shown a marble plaque bearing the names of the club's past presidents, which read like a roll call of Avadh's best-known Taluqdar families.

My second invitation was from an entirely different kind of place.

I was an honoured guest once again, but what a strange setting it was! When I reached the venue, the iron gates were barred and shut. Two frightening-looking guards with bristling moustaches eyed me suspiciously as I looked around nervously. Was this still a part of Lucknow? Scrub forest stretched as far as I could see and an eerie stillness beat against my eardrums. Even the sky that stretched above, infected by the miserable lives inside, had a dull, grey pall. The trees around had leaves, yes, but they were a sickly yellow, limp and listless. A nearby grove of mangoes stood motionless, not a leaf stirring, and I was sure that no koel ever sang there. My reverie was broken by the harsh cry of the brain-fever bird as it screeched across the sky. I moved forward slowly and looked apprehensively at the guards.

The guards caught hold of the heavy iron bars and slowly opened the doors to reveal a knot of women prisoners waiting eagerly to greet me and I was immediately surrounded by their affectionate greetings.

Fate, circumstances and social laws had wrapped these lives in their coils to thrust them into a world where youth, love, desire and hope were barred from entering. However hard I looked, there was neither joy nor hope in the faces before me. These were women grown old before their time: the young looked like middle-aged crones and the older ones were like walking corpses. Expressionless eyes stared at me in the hall where we sat; I felt the piercing gaze of a hundred and eighty pairs of eyes bore into me. I looked around to look at individual faces. Each woman was clean, neatly dressed, obedient and silent – and I felt as if a garland of flowers had been placed around my neck by the reverence I saw in their eyes as they stared at me. Who could say that these faces were placed on necks that had barely escaped a noose!

'Most of them are murderers,' the doctor informed me as if she had heard my unspoken question. 'Some are here on charges of dacoity or armed robbery. Not one of them is here for anything less. Often the ones who are sent here are those whose death sentences have been commuted.'

Lunch had been served on a table for the doctor and me, and the women, like well-trained soldiers, had sat down behind small slabs of cement that served as chowkis. Their faces showed little interest in the food before them.

'The entire meal has been cooked by them,' the doctor went on, and I looked carefully at the feast before me. I tried to suppress the vision of a pair of hands severing a head with a hatchet. Before me were deliciously puffed puris, khasta kachoris, the kind of pumpkin sabzi without which the richness of a khasta kachori is incomplete, raita, chutney. Each dish was more delicious than the other. I wondered when they had last had a meal like this served to them on their thalis.

And then my eye fell on one who looked at the food in front of her with no delight. Had the aroma of the ghee-soaked food awakened some memories that had robbed her appetite? A wedding feast, a mundan or a family puja, perhaps, when the kitchen at home overflowed with the fragrant smells from the pots and pans. Was the memory of that occasion choking her now?

'Come on, start eating, otherwise they won't eat.' The doctor's smiling voice brought me back to the present. I broke a piece of a puri and, immediately, all the women started to eat.

The kind-hearted doctor had brought about several changes in these drab lives. From time to time, she would invite guests to meet the prisoners. And her research work was dedicated to studying their behaviour. She had mingled her heartbeat with those of the hundred and eighty prisoners that she monitored. By now, she knew their bodies as well as she knew their minds and had the histories of each one at her fingertips. Their lives were like well-thumbed books that she read and re-read almost every day.

'The one who is fanning you,' she said, 'her name is Heera. She must be about fifty-eight or so, but if you had seen her dance last year at the Independence Day function, you would have been amazed. She could put to shame any twenty-year-old!' I looked up to see this Salome, and her lined and withered face broke into a sweet smile. When she was not fanning me, she ran to fetch me hot puris from the kitchen and, no matter how much I dissuaded her from piling more on my thali, she would slip another hot one in. When I finished my meal, she ran to fetch a basin and jug of water and made me wash my hands as if I were a child. Then, before I knew what she was up to, she drank the water from the basin.

'Stop!' I cried in horror. 'What are you doing?'

'Bahuji' – she looked into my eyes – 'my burden of sins is so heavy that I can hardly hold my head upright. This water from the hands of good women like yourself is not dirty water, bahuji, it is like gangajal to sinners like us. It may wash my past away.'

I returned to the table and asked the doctor to tell me more about Heera; I was stunned by what I heard. The woman who had drunk 'gangajal' today had helped her son burn alive his young wife. The son had been sent to the gallows, but she had been given a life sentence and left alone to be forever haunted by the noose that had killed her son.

The doctor next pointed out a dark young girl with sad eyes. She was innocent in the sense that she had committed no heinous crime herself, but she was guilty of assisting her three brothers in committing armed robberies. Now, she was the unofficial seamstress of the jail and would be sorely missed by her fellow inmates when her term came to an end, the doctor went on. Her nimble fingers crocheted complicated roses and flowers and her knack for transforming the drab prison uniform into something else was widely appreciated. Give her a shapeless vest, and she would add a tuck there and a pleat here to make it into a sexy body stocking.

I knew that the minute a woman enters a prison she is stripped of all her jewellery and personal clothing and issued a coarse dhoti-kurti. Yet, these women had devised all kinds of ways of adding a touch of individuality to their uniform. I had been struck earlier by the absence of any mirrors – for most women this must be a fate worse than death. Yet, every woman had neatly parted hair, some had a black bindi on their foreheads and even a hint of kajal in their eyes. How had they managed this without a mirror, I wondered. Then the secret was revealed to me. I saw a tall, strapping woman bent over a pail of water. She looked at her reflection in the water and patted her hair. Obviously, not even the grim confines of a prison can quash a woman's vanity! The doctor told me how they made kajal from burnt wood, crushed coals to make missi to fill the spaces between their teeth and cut rose petals to fashion a bindi.

After the meal, I went with the doctor on a round of the cells. The sun was shining outside, but a pall of silence and suffocating darkness seemed to envelop the rooms. The windows had thick iron bars and the sky had shrunk so far that it was just a hint of blue-grey. I could well imagine how they must crane their necks to see more of it before their eyes, tired of squinting, gave up the effort. The large dormitory had a long, depressing row of cement slabs, not unlike those that you see in a morgue. Each one had neatly rolled-up bedding of rough blankets. The walls had '*Raghu Pati Raghav Raja Ram, Patit Pavan Sita Ram*' painted in bold lettering all along the room. Did these lines provide solace to souls tossing restlessly at night? Or did these words strike out like a hooded snake to remind them of all they had done? The neck of a husband severed for a lover, a daughter-in-law burnt alive, the rape and pillage of a dacoity, the selling of young girls to pimps and prostitutes, the killing of newborn girls . . .

Until a few months ago, two sisters-in-law were incarcerated together in this jail, I was told. Both were serving a life sentence, but their visceral hatred of each other became so hard to handle that one had to be packed off to Naini Jail near Allahabad. 'I was afraid they would kill each other one day,' the doctor said. And then I was told of the strange saga of their feud. For years, the older one had watched her brother-in-law lavish attention on his young wife. He was prosperous and she loved clothes and jewellery. Each time he gave her a new gift, she came to her older sister-in-law and showed it off. Finally, the older one could take it no more. She decided to hack off the neck that was draped with the jewels that she coveted; she would have been given the death sentence were it not for the infant at her breast. The mother and baby were sent here. According to the rules of the time, a child could stay with its mother until the age of six. In the meantime, her brother-in-law married his dead wife's sister. When the son turned six, he was sent back to his father's house. The child became very attached to his new aunt, who loved him in turn.

Then, one day, the child's mother arrived home on parole. The son refused to go to her and clung to his aunt's sari. Burning with rage, the mother felt as if her new sister-in-law had grown another head to replace the one she had hacked all those years ago. As the time for her return to jail drew nearer, she felt more and more enraged and helpless. Her frustration had added a wicked edge to her tongue and her family began to dread the lashings they received from her. She turned to her new enemy one day.

'I'll hack your neck just as I hacked your sister's off,

understand? I'll come from jail if I have to,' she spat. 'Don't you dare charm my little Nanku away from me! You think I haven't seen you slyly feeding him milk and jalebis to wean him away from me? I know you will kill him one day.' The child, who was listening to this exchange, blanched when he heard his mother. From that day, he wouldn't go close to his aunt. His mother had barely reached jail after her parole when she was told that her son had been hacked to death by her sister-in-law.

This is how they both found themselves in the same jail, serving life sentences. Forced to see each other every day was a predicament harder than the sentence itself. Finally, the older one was packed off to Naini Jail. With her arch enemy gone, the younger one began to be haunted by the crime she had committed.

'Why didn't they send me to the gallows instead?' she would wail. 'Every night, the little one comes to my ears and calls out: "Chachi, O Chachi!"'

I was told that the room where she killed her little nephew was so dark that the police had to carry burning torches to collect the pieces of the child's body.

Yet, the same jail also housed those who were completely unrepentant. The doctor took me to a cell where a tall woman, Najmati, stood proudly alone. Her arms were decorously crossed in front of her and she looked briefly at us as we entered, then turned her gaze away. What glowing skin she had, and what a nose! Perhaps her haughty and irreverent attitude was responsible for her being excluded from this morning's feast. That brief glance she had cast at us had shaken me – she looked like a barely controlled lioness at a circus, who could jump and trap you between her jaws if the ringmaster lost control. Her tawny eyes burnt with an anger that sent a shiver down my spine. I stood hesitantly at the door of her cell as if she were a maharani and I had dared to intrude into her private chamber.

At first glance, she appeared to be about twenty or so, but when I looked closely, I realized she was older. I saw her look slyly at us and assess me exactly as I was assessing her. 'So,' she seemed to say silently, 'seen enough, have you? Are you satisfied with the specimens you've seen at this zoo?' She flashed a defiant grin my way, dazzling me with her missi-laced teeth and tawny eyes. Then, she rudely turned her back on us and withdrew to her own world.

'What a beauty she must have been in her youth!' I told the doctor as we moved on.

'I wish her life had been half as beautiful,' the doctor replied. 'God knows how many lives she helped extinguish, how many happy families she destroyed – she was the moll of a gang of dacoits. You should see the visitors she gets! One of them is a young Thakur boy: he had come the other day with a basket full of dry fruits for her. No one is allowed to keep so many, I said. You can only bring her as much as she can eat while sitting here. So he flashed me a wicked grin and fed her the whole lot in one go!' The doctor laughed. I was reminded suddenly of a story I was once told of a Pathan who was travelling on a train with his ram: when he was asked to buy a ticket for the ram, he cut it up and ate it there and then!

'Wait till you meet this one.' My doctor friend smiled as we walked on. My appetite had been whetted by her enthusiasm and we strode towards the kitchen, a poky little room, full of woodsmoke. Two tall, strapping women were frying puris in a huge wok and my eyes almost missed a third person hidden by the swirling smoke. She got up and joined her hands in greeting, and the doctor said heartily: 'This lady is from your part of the world, Chanuli.' Chanuli blushed as she turned to face me.

'So, Chanuli, what is your village called?' I asked her in Kumaoni. Little did I know that the sound of her mother tongue would undo the floodgates of a past that Chanuli tried to erase as she cooked for her fellow prisoners. She covered her face with both her hands and sobbed into them as if her heart would break. I felt unable to say or do anything and looked to the doctor for help.

'She has heard her own dialect after so long that she could not control herself, poor thing,' the doctor said kindly. 'I have never seen her cry like this before.' Then she turned to Chanuli and said, 'Come on, Chanuli, I have some work for you. Take this lady on a round of the jail and show her the school, all right?'

Chanuli tried to regain her composure. She wiped her eyes with her pallu and then turned politely to me. 'Please follow me,' she said. I followed her wordlessly through the jail to the school. My heart felt as if it would break as I saw the rows of children sitting in their class, for they were like no other children I knew. The face of a six-year-old had the eyes of a person twenty years older studded on it. The joyless faces twinkled briefly as they saw us approach, almost like the fading glow of a flashlight, and then the sparkle was snuffed out once again. They were asked to recite poems for me, and they went through the motions mechanically, their voices rising and falling and their little hands describing arcs and circles as if they were clockwork toys that had been wound up to perform. I remembered the Rajasthani puppets I had seen as a child, whose puppeteer used to beat an old tin can to keep the beat: the puppets slashed at each other in mock battle and then arose once again to play another story, another character.

These children – all under six, the age till when they were allowed to stay with their mothers – were forced into a life where they had no place. What kindness did the framers of this rule have in mind when they forced these innocent souls to start their life's journey inside the four walls of a prison?

I could not bear to stay there any longer. Suddenly, the doctor appeared again. 'Perhaps you would like to speak to Chanuli alone,' she said thoughtfully and led me out. I went into a clean, spartan cell and Chanuli came and sat obediently near my feet, as if she were my pet cat. We were silent for some time: where could I begin, and where could she start her story? I looked at her face once again, struck by its pristine innocence. How could someone like her have murdered anyone? And then she started to tell me the strange story of her life.

Far in the Uttaranchal area of Kumaon, there were two villages close to each other: one was Chanuli's father's village and the other her father-in-law's. Her husband saw the pretty Chanuli grazing her father's flock of goats on the terraced fields of her village and fell in love with her. His mother never forgave him for choosing his own bride and refused to accept Chanuli as her daughter-in-law. Their daily fights became the favourite entertainment of the village and the entire community participated in their angry verbal battles. To add to her misery, the Indo-Chinese war broke out soon after Chanuli was married and her husband was called to the border.

He never returned.

Her son's death turned her mother-in-law mad with grief and she turned the full force of her fury on poor Chanuli: 'Kulachchini, you cursed creature,' she yelled, 'you are the cause of my son's death!' The old woman turned into a human cannon and spewed abuses at Chanuli night and day. One day, as soon as Chanuli took a new sickle and went to the jungle to gather fodder for the cattle, she was followed by a gang of women from the village. 'Look at her' – their taunts followed her as she walked – 'does she behave like a widow? She still wears her mangalsutra and her nose-ring – a whore! That's what she is! No wonder the old woman curses her, what else can she do but rue her fate if this is the daughter-in-law she's got!' Chanuli had refused to discard her mangalsutra and her nose-ring after she had heard of the death of her husband and this had led to her being virtually ostracized by the village women.

'I swear, Didi' – she looked at me with her clear eyes – 'my heart told me he was still alive. My heart never lies,

Didi, so how could I take off the mangalsutra he had placed there? I had dreamt of him the previous night and my heart was so heavy that something snapped inside me when that woman called me a whore. I flung my sickle at her in anger. How was I to know, Didi, that her neck would be severed with that one fling?'

I looked at her wide eyes, – and I tell you that if I were the judge to whom she had said this, I would have freed her there and then. Such clear eyes can only belong to an innocent heart. We both fell silent.

'What happened then?' I asked her gently, after a while.

'It was as if a fountain of blood was spouting. I ran home in terror. But everyone had seen what happened. That night, I was taken to Almora.'

'Did anyone post your bail?' I asked.

'Who would do that?' She sighed deeply. 'I was guilty of killing someone, of a Brahma-hatya. She was a Brahmin, you know,' she explained. 'Only my mother wailed and ran after the bus in which they took me for as long as she could.'

There was a pause. Then she continued: 'They registered a case. The only question they asked me over and over again was: "Did you throw that sickle?" And I would answer: "Yes." Then you know that you committed a murder, they would say, and I would reply: "No, sahib, I did not kill anyone, it was an accident."'

She reached out and held my hand. 'Tell me, Didi,' she said to me now, 'I did not kill her deliberately, don't you see? It just happened!' I wish I could tell you how innocent and guileless she sounded as she said 'It just happened!' to me in Kumaoni. How I wished I had been the judge for this case!

Her gaze was as pure as the Bhagirathi river that flows through our part of the world. She still blushed as she recounted the heady days of her brief honeymoon with her husband. It seemed to me as if her childlike innocence was enough to clear the gloom of this hateful place. She was not just the prettiest prisoner, she was also the one who had the sweetest temperament. They had started a Girl Guides movement in the jail and Chanuli showed me her uniform proudly. Unfortunately, neither her beauty nor her touching innocence was enough to absolve her of her crime. Yet, I knew that no hangman would ever find the courage to slip a noose round her neck.

She was sent first to Naini and then transferred to Lucknow. Then, somewhere along the way, like the plot of a bad Bombay film, her husband came back from war, miraculously alive. He ran from pillar to post to free his young bride. He appealed in the High Court, saying that if she were freed, he would take her back. His wife was blameless, she had been provoked by the village women, was his appeal. All the world loves a lover, and the High Court reduced her life imprisonment to four years. He used to write to her regularly.

'Did he ever come and visit you?' I asked.

'No, his mother would not allow him,' she replied. 'If he came here, to this polluted place, he would have to feed the whole village as penance. But his letters . . .' She suddenly broke off, blushed and buried her face in her knees. I guessed that the letters were passionate enough for her to live in hope. 'There has not been a letter for these last two years,' she whispered. 'And one day my elder brother-in-law came here.'

'Did you ask him why?'

'How could I, Didi?' she asked in shocked tones. 'I was too shy to speak to him.'

I could only stare at her pale face. For her, the fact that her husband had appealed on her behalf was reason enough to go on living.

'I know he must have remarried by now, Didi,' she went on. 'I keep thinking, I have already spent two years of my sentence, only two more remain. But where will I go after that? If I ever meet him, this is what I want to ask him: "If you were never going to take me home, why did you fight for my sentence to be reduced?" This prison is now my only refuge, Didi. It is my mother's home and my husband's. When I came here, I did not know how to read and write. Now I do. The days pass in my daily chores, but it is the nights that haunt me. In Chaitra, I keep remembering the ripe kaphal berries of my village, and how every home must be preparing a basket of bhaintuli to send to their married daughters. In Baisakh, I remember the apples, the apricots, and in Magh-Pusa, the snowfalls. There are nights on end when I dream of snow falling softly . . .'

'Chanuli, if I go to the hills this year, I promise you I'll visit your village,' I told her. 'You said your village is just two hours from Almora. What was the name? And what is your father's name?'

The dreams of snow vanished and the trees laden with apples and apricots withered under my question. She went pale. 'Why name a village that has ostracized me, Didi?' she replied. 'I have shamed my father, and I swore the day they took me away that I would never show him my face as long as I lived, nor bring the name of the village to my lips. But there are some landmarks that I can tell you about. My father is a Brahmin and the village headman. He wears a brown tweed coat and black pyjamas. His spectacles have only half a frame, the other side is held up by a loop of thread around his ear. There is a path on the right side of my house that descends straight from the Shiva temple into our courtyard. And there are three pear trees in front of my house. Behind it is a huge walnut tree.' She described the geography of her whole village to me in graphic detail and looked at me hopefully. Then, to make it clearer still, she said, 'My father-in-law is a very quiet man and my husband's younger brother looks exactly like him, only he is fairer. They haven't done his thread ceremony as yet, so he wears his hair in two long plaits.'

She looked at me again and asked softly, 'You will be able to find them, won't you, Didi?'

What could I say? Where in all of Uttaranchal would I find a headman who wears a brown tweed coat and black pyjamas, with a thread looped over one ear to keep his spectacles in place? And if I did, would I be able to give him a message from his weeping daughter? In all the houses scattered on the mountains of Kumaon, where should I find a house that has a path descending from the temple into its courtyard, one which has three pear trees in front and a walnut tree in the backyard? And would I ever find the young brother-in-law who was a fairer version of a man I had never met?

'Anything else?' I asked her helplessly.

'Yes, Didi,' she went on eagerly and pulled me along on the journey from her village to the kutchery in Almora. 'After you've met my family, go to the kutchery in Almora and do me a favour. When they took me to Almora, they stripped me of my jewellery. I refused to part with my charyo – mangalsutra – but when they made me unscrew my nose-ring, I began to cry. I begged them with folded hands and the Patwarijyu said, "You silly girl, who cares for auspicious and inauspicious omens in a jail? Are you the first woman who has been asked to remove her jewellery? Even a queen would have to do the same." They took my nose-ring and placed it on a stone. I fell at his feet – you know what a bad omen it is to keep a mark of your suhaag on a stone?'

Of course I knew. No married woman is allowed to keep a mangalsutra, nose-ring or glass bangles on a stone surface. In fact, one of the worst curses you can hurl at a married woman is: 'May your charyo be kept on a stone!'

'The Patwarijyu then told me that they will enter all these items into a register and keep them safely. Don't cry, he told me. So, please, Didi, please go and make sure with your own eyes they have indeed kept my nose-ring safely, will you?'

I don't know how I had managed to keep back my tears

through this sad story, but now the dam threatened to burst. Her husband had abandoned Chanuli, her village had ostracized her, but she had never given up hope of wearing that nose-ring again! How many men have such devoted wives, I wondered.

I tried to change the topic and said, 'I'm told you sing beautifully, Chanuli. I haven't heard a pahari song for a long time. Won't you sing one for me?'

Her eyes lit up and then she turned her gaze down shyly. 'I hear you sang a lovely one at the Independence Day celebrations recently,' I coaxed her like I would a shy child. Won't you sing it for me?'

And then the clear tone of a pahari flute rang in my ears as she sang:

Paltano ko bajo bajana lagyo
Jhola tamtola sajan lagyo
O meri Ija, pakey de kheera
Ladan sun janchcho Kumaiyya veera . . .

The sounds of the war drums can be heard
And the army is dressed in its uniform and weapons.
O Mother, quickly cook some kheer
For the brave Kumaoni soldier who is off to fight for
his country . . .

Chanuli sang on, her eyes closed for the soldier she had once seen leave. The hot loo blowing outside turned for a brief while into the cool mountain breeze of our Kumaon and I was riding a bus to Nainital from Almora. We were driving through the Kakrighat valley with the Himalayas spread before us. The bus was full of passengers with crates of apples from their orchards and it reeked of the slightly sour smell of ripe apples. Sometimes, the sound of a plaintive flute being played reached my ears and I could hear '*Paltano ko bajo . . .*'

I came back to earth with a thud: I could sense we were no longer alone in the room. Chanuli's sweet voice had dragged in an audience of prisoners and the room was full of silent listeners. I looked at the faces that had seemed so grim that morning – now, they were coloured with sadness as a wave of nostalgia ran through us all. But the spell was broken and I rose to leave.

'Won't you say a few words to them before you go?' the doctor asked me.

I shook my head; what could I say? I looked deep into their eyes, bid a silent goodbye to each one of them and left.

The open sky seemed vast and cruel after the confined spaces I had been cooped up in all day. I turned to look one last time, but the heavy iron gates had been closed. A small window was open and I could feel two tearful eyes follow me.

'Two years more, Didi, then where will I go?' Her voice rang continually in my ears. Years ago, the blind folk singer Kalu had sung a haunting song for us at Santiniketan. Chanuli's eyes brought back that song:

Chhina shikal paye niye ore pakhi
Ja ude, ja ude, ja re ekaki . . .

Carry the broken chains dangling from your legs,
O bird,
And fly away, fly away, fly away alone . . .

Janaki

How strange, I thought, that a woman whose name was Janaki had no trace of the goddess she was named after. This Janaki had conspired with her lover to kill her own husband. I awaited her arrival impatiently, although this time I was not alone. The prison's security staff was present and I wondered whether she would be willing to speak freely to me in their presence. After all, when two women exchange confidences, have they ever wished for an audience?

It was the first navratri of Chaitra and I had chosen to spend it in a prison. They say that since this is the first day of the Hindu year, the rest of the year takes its lead from what happens on that day. I had already heard of Janaki's story, but I was now keen to meet her and hear it from her own lips. She entered silently and I was startled to see her suddenly loom before me. I gestured at her to sit down and my glance swept from her face to the hands placed on her knees. If her face had been covered and I'd only seen those wrists, I would have mistaken them for a young man's muscular hands. One swipe from them could fell someone easily, I thought to myself. But the rest of her was unmistakably feminine: skin like ripe wheat and a tight, voluptuous body. There was no trace of the pallor so common to inmates: her face was flushed with a healthy, rosy glow. She kept her glance averted, though, and her thick lashes kept her eyes hidden from my gaze. Gandhiji had said that every crime is written on the criminal's face, but this one was firmly shuttered. Her expression was carefully neutral: neither joy nor sorrow, nor a nervous twitch, to give her thoughts away.

Our shastras say: '*Punyo vai punyain karmana bhavati, papah papeneti*' (Good deeds make a man virtuous and sins a sinner). What had made her a sinner? What prompted her to lead the man she had married to her lover's hatchet? Why had she conspired to kill her husband?

I had been told that this young woman, sitting so politely in front of me today, with her eyes modestly downcast, had hidden her young lover for two days in a dark room in her house. The young man had a sharp hatchet ready. She had coaxed her husband into the dark room and the two lovers then cut him into little pieces, as if he were a stalk of sugarcane. I looked at her face closely, but I could find no trace of emotion in that carefully composed face.

'I have come to hear your story from your own lips.' I smiled at her.

She looked up then and smiled in return. Nothing had

prepared me for that smile. I'd had no idea that the memory I was trying to uncover would evoke anything like a smile from her. I had been preparing myself for a long sigh, even a burst of tears – but a smile? Her cheeks dimpled and secret happiness spread over her shining face. Her teeth flashed briefly at me and I was charmed by them. How long had it been since she had smiled like that? When she came here, hounded by the press and her neighbours, her own seven-year-old was reported to have said: '*Chhi, Mummy, tum gandi ho*!' (Ugh, Mummy, you're disgusting!)

I wonder what had prompted the little girl's disgust: had she suddenly woken up to see her father lying in a pool of blood? Or had she seen her mother making a cup of tea for an 'uncle' she had once spotted in that dark room?

'Who is he?' she had asked her mother.

'He's your uncle, child,' the mother had answered calmly.

'No, he's not!' she had said vehemently. 'Ugh, Mummy, you're disgusting!'

When I reminded her of her daughter's words, Janaki's smile suddenly vanished. She shrank into a shell and her neck disappeared into her shoulders. So the smile was just a mask, I realized. She had retreated from me and it was futile to proceed with questions about the past, for it was obvious that she had no wish to reopen old wounds. Haunted by the memories of the articles in newspapers, the lawyers' and her own family's accusations, she had decided to become an unfeeling iceberg. She had left all her modesty and guilt outside the walls of the prison and the smile she had flashed at me when we first met came from the persona she had adopted inside the prison to survive.

An oppressive silence filled the room; both of us were loath to break it. Ultimately, I decided to chip away at the iceberg.

'Do you ever regret what you did, Janaki?' I asked her.

She looked up then, startled and angry, stung like a cobra when the snake-charmer provokes it to come out from its basket with his nudge, and I almost recoiled at the anger in those eyes. Her eyes were red and fairly sparking with fire now.

'Regret what, may I ask?' she retorted. 'What have I done?'

I felt like asking: if you are so innocent, have you come here on a pilgrimage?

But she lowered her head once more and then slowly began to speak.

I watched her face carefully, fascinated by the expressions that were rapidly chasing each other, like the changing colours of a chameleon as it moves along a branch. She was sometimes coy, then she trembled with anger; occasionally, she rubbed her hands together in frustration and beads of perspiration started to collect on her forehead. But never once did she falter – her tongue was like that of a woman possessed, it carried on speaking, and her voice rose and fell rhythmically as she recounted her life.

Not many editors would have the stomach to go through her script, I can assure you. And yet, in a sense, her story was ageless, a script that the world has heard and rewritten so many times. She was born in a prosperous farmer's family in Punjab and reached puberty rather early. Her face was not especially beautiful, but there was a robust health that shone through her young body. Ripe red lips, merry, sparkling eyes and a firm, voluptuous body. It was probably all that milk and honey that gave her cheeks that flush, I reflected, even here where roses on cheeks wither within days. Her eyes were not ringed by dark circles, nor did her lips look dry and chapped.

Her calm, unhurried voice proceeded with her story: She was happy growing up in her father's home, running through the wheat fields and raiding the mango groves in summer, when she heard that a prospective groom's family was coming to see her. She was dressed in a clean set of clothes for the occasion and taken in to be shown to the boy's older brother, who had come to assess the new bride for his younger brother. Janaki's father had made generous arrangements for the emissary; a tall glass of fresh buttermilk, homemade sweets made from the milk of their own buffaloes and several other delicacies had been prepared for the groom's party. Finally, Janaki was led into the room.

Her prospective brother-in-law's jaw dropped open at the sight of her fresh, young body and he decided to accept her father's proposal, not for his younger brother but for himself. He was a bachelor and had, in a rash moment, declared he would never marry as long as he lived, but now he was willing to break that vow of celibacy. Janaki was just sixteen and he was forty-eight years old – yet, neither her father nor her mother objected, overjoyed as they were to have such a prosperous man bid for their daughter's hand. In any case, he did not look a day over forty, they told her. Look at his bushy moustache, and not a single grey hair on his head still! Tall, strapping and handsome – they wished for nothing more for their daughter.

That night, Janaki sobbed into her pillow as she reflected on what lay in store for her. How could she possibly believe in the honesty of a man who had cheated his younger brother? How sacred did he consider his vow of celibacy if he broke it the first time he met an attractive woman? God knows how many other women he would lust for. When she reached her husband's home and was introduced to his younger brother, Janaki was devastated: this was the man she could have married if his older brother had not snatched her away, she thought despairingly.

But it was too late to change her life.

Meanwhile, her husband outdid himself in lavishing his attention on his new bride: she had to merely mention a sweet she craved before he produced it. He loaded her with glittering new clothes and jewellery – all that he thought would win her heart. However, there was another, darker side to him that Janaki occasionally saw: he had a fearful temper and was jealously possessive about her. If he ever caught her smiling or talking to another man, he became livid, and if Janaki joked or laughed with his younger brother, his eyes turned red with rage and a terrible battle erupted. Naturally, over time, her husband's obsessive jealousy destroyed their relationship. She had produced three healthy children in these five years and excelled in cooking, sewing and embroidery. Her house shone like a mirror and she got up at the crack of dawn and finished her chores before waking the children to get them ready for school. Yet, nothing she did ever brought a smile to her husband's sour face.

'Was he here again yesterday?' he'd ask, and she would stand silently.

How could she lie? Wasn't this his own brother's house and wasn't he free to visit his family when he wanted? Yet, she knew that if, for the sake of peace, she lied, she would have to tell many more to cover that one up. The servants, the children – after all, how many mouths could she keep shut?

'I've told you a hundred times,' her husband yelled, 'that bastard must never come here! Why can't you listen to me? Do you want to die one day at my hands?' Little did he know that he would die one day at her hands.

But what was he like, I asked Janaki, this man who defied his brother's anger and came to visit her at his peril? And why did she never put her foot down firmly? After all, she must have realized that her husband did not make idle threats – she herself had told me how many times he had thrashed her and flung food in her face. The walls would tremble at his rage, she'd told me, and the neighbours would shamelessly eavesdrop, whispering: 'There they go again!' to each other when the pots and pans flew in Janaki's house. She looked up then and started on the next chapter of her life.

'He used to live next door to us, ji,' she began. 'He was then in the twelfth class and weak in English. He used to come over to study in peace to our house. He called me Behenji and I called him Bhaiyya.'

She fell silent again. I waited for her to go on. I was now a surgeon and she the patient spread before me. My knife hovered over her body. How many so-called sisters have eloped with their 'brothers', I reflected, covering their real feelings with the socially acceptable relationship of a brother and sister? A school friend of mine used to tie a rakhi on a 'brother' for years and he sent her a money order from wherever he was. Then, many years later, I ran into them again. There were three children with them, and they called her 'brother' 'Daddy'! 'Are these your children?' I asked her, and she had the grace to blush.

Anyway, Janaki was not the first girl who had redefined a relationship, I thought. On the one hand was a jealous, hot-tempered husband. On the other was a gentle, loving youth, closer to her in every respect than the older man she was married to, who came every morning to study and gaze at her lovingly. She made him tea and he smiled sweetly to thank her. She had no idea when her feelings for her brother-in-law changed. Soon, he began to learn other lessons from her as well. Then one day, when Janaki's husband returned unexpectedly and saw his wife lovingly brewing tea for his younger brother, he was livid. 'If I ever catch you in my house again,' he told his trembling brother, 'I'll shoot you on sight!'

Strangely, this only made the lovers more defiant and

they continued to meet on the sly. Finally, they decided that this Othello had to be killed. The brother-in-law sharpened his hatchet and showed her how sharp it was by touching it with his finger. Blood immediately spouted from the cut. See? This is how sharp its mere touch is, he told her. Imagine what will happen if I slice off his neck.

'I hid him in a dark storeroom, ji,' Janaki told me. 'We had planned to kill my husband that night. Then, I don't know why but the old man wouldn't settle down. He kept saying: "I have a strange feeling, there's someone hiding here to kill me."' Talk of omens and portents: I have always believed that death never comes unannounced; only you must know how to read the signs.

'That night' – Janaki's tale continued – 'he wouldn't let me sleep either. Morning came and he went off to his office. It was the first of the month, who knows, maybe he lived on to collect another month's wage . . .' She sighed deeply.

'So did your lover spend the night thirsty and hungry in the storeroom?' I asked her.

'Of course not,' she replied. 'I had slipped him some dinner, and when I gave my children their usual bedtime glass of milk, I gave him one as well. He was nervous in that dark room, so I spent some time with him, giving him courage.' I was dying to ask what that meant, but the plot was too complex now to meander into subplots. 'That night, when my husband returned, he was roaring drunk. He always got the children lots of sweets and things on pay day, and that day too, the basket on his cycle was laden with gifts for them.'

'Oh, so he loved them did he?' I couldn't help interjecting.

'Of course.' She looked up. 'Which father does not love his children? He loved me too.' For the first time, I understood the meaning of these lines:

> *Vidihi na nari hridaya gati jani*
> *Sakal kapat adh avguna khani*
>
> No one can fathom a woman's heart
> She is a mine of wiles

I almost blushed in shame for her.

'He'd bought some mutton home that day,' Janaki carried on. 'I was furious when he asked me to cook it for dinner. I told him: "It is nine o'clock, when will I grind the masalas and when will I cook it? I've already cooked dinner for tonight. I'll cook it tomorrow. In any case, the children have gone to bed." But he refused to listen to me. "No, cook it now," he ordered. I also stuck to my argument, and each time he said now, I would say tomorrow. Finally, I gave in, but I was livid with anger. I cooked the mutton but couldn't eat it because I was so furious. I wept that night before I went to bed and slept so deeply that I was dead to the world. Then I felt his hand on my shoulder, shaking me awake. "What's happened?" I asked. "Come here," he ordered. I did not want to sleep with him, but I knew that if I refused him, he would start to yell and abuse me: the children would wake up and the neighbours would hear us. So I went. It was well past midnight when I returned to my bed. For a moment, I felt I should go and check the storeroom, but I didn't have the nerve – suppose the old man got up? I thought. Let him sleep for a while, and then I'll go.'

Then she fell silent.

The silence lengthened into something different, and I felt as if I was watching a play being re-enacted. On the stage is a bed with the head of the household spread-eagled across it. It is the first of the month, he has had his favourite dinner of mutton curry and chapatis and made love to his wife and there is a contented smile on his face. On the adjoining bed lies his wife, and between them is their little son, his sleeping form spanning them like a bridge of love. On the third bed are their two daughters. The older one is her father's favourite, but he loves the little one too. There is a box of sweets for each of them placed so that they see it first thing in the morning when they wake up. It is the last gift they will ever get from their father.

The only eyewitness to the grisly crime that took place that night was the ceiling fan whirring overhead. When Janaki was sure that her husband was fast asleep, she wondered if she should tiptoe to the storeroom. 'Then I felt as if someone was standing over my head,' she said. 'I was still a little dazed after the events of the past few hours. I sat up hurriedly and saw him.

'"What are you doing here?" I whispered. "Go! Run quickly. If he gets up he'll kill both of us!"

'"Who will kill us?" He grinned, and my blood ran cold. "O god, o god," I said and looked at the other bed. There was blood everywhere – it had formed a pool under the bed and even spattered the blades of the overhead fan as it must have gushed out like a fountain when his neck was hacked. I felt his neck was rising from his head, ji' – Janaki looked at me in terror – 'and I flung my sheet and ran outside. He followed me there.

'"What have you done?" I asked him. "What will happen to us now?"

'And he said, "Why worry? We'll deal with whatever happens together. Now listen to me carefully: go and clean the blood quickly and then fetch me a large trunk."

'"A large trunk? Whatever for?" I asked him.

'"See that goods train there? It always stands there for about two hours. We'll heave his body into it and . . . "

'I was weeping in terror by now. "No, no, I can't do this," I said.

'"Look," he told me firmly. "There is no time to waste. You can't weep and howl now. We have hardly any time left. Go and swab the floor with your dupatta and I'll go and have a bath and wash off all the blood. It's bloody cold," he muttered as he headed towards our bathroom.

'"There is a tap with hot water there," I told him. "Go and bathe under that; I'll make us some tea."

Her husband's body was still bleeding and Janaki lit the stove to make some tea. The blood began to congeal on the floor. She cleaned it off and gathered the clots in her dupatta while her children – of the same flesh and blood – slept peacefully. Then she got her lover a fresh change of clothes from her husband's cupboard. The clever boy had stripped to his underwear before the murder so that no telltale bloodstained clothes gave him away. Neither of them saw the hundreds of bloodstains that had spattered every part of the room – the walls, the fan, the floor. They stuffed his body into a tin trunk and were heading for the train when the smell of milk burning on the stove woke her elder daughter. 'Mummy, did Daddy break your bottle of bindi again last night?' she asked. Janaki quickly ran her eye over the room: where had she forgotten to swab the blood? Then the girl spotted a man lurking in the dark kitchen. 'Who is that, Mummy?' she asked. He had covered his face, but who was wearing her father's clothes and where was her father?

'This is your uncle, child,' Janaki replied as calmly as she could.

'No!' the child screamed. 'He is not my uncle! You are disgusting, Mummy!'

Janaki slapped her and shut the door to the kitchen. The two of them tried to complete their unfinished task.

'You go.' Janaki was panicking now. 'I'll deal with this end.'

'No,' he said firmly. 'I won't leave you alone.' But she managed to persuade him and handed him her husband's bicycle, transistor, wristwatch and his precious terylene shirts.

'Take these and leave this town immediately,' she instructed him.

'But why did you hand him all that?' I asked.

'The minute the news of his death spread, his other

brothers would descend on the house and take his things away,' Janaki replied. 'I didn't want that!' She looked at me as if I was foolish to even ask the question that had such an obvious answer. I was completely nonplussed, I have to say. What was she, this woman who bared her whole story to me so innocently? A witch or a child?

Her brother-in-law left, but not before he told her what to do. 'Open all the doors as you always do in the mornings,' he told her. 'Get up at your usual time, neither before nor after. Then scream and faint. Don't weep, understand? Then people will think it was a dacoit who came and murdered your husband.'

She did exactly as she was told: she screamed, fainted and then fell silent. Then, three days later, they brought her lover in front of her. He was handcuffed and she could carry on the charade no longer. She confessed everything.

'I could not stop myself, ji,' she apologized to me. And I remembered:

Tiriya jal maha aag lagave
Tiriya sukhe naav chalave.

A woman who can set fire to water is also
The who can row a boat over sand

This woman did not shed a tear when her husband died, and yet, she broke down when she saw her lover in chains.

'Don't cry,' he told her. 'I've put an end to all your sorrows, haven't I?'

They are both in adjoining jails now, but they have never been further apart, each haunted by memories.

Janaki remembers the wheat fields in her father's village, the day her husband came to see her and the day, just three days after she had been married, when Janaki had caught her husband in bed with his elder sister-in-law.

'Shocked, are you?' The older woman had grinned at her horrified face. 'This has been happening since before you were born!'

Yet, when she turned for solace to his younger brother, he almost threw her out.

Nor can she forget her youngest child, the son she adored. 'That night, he was sleeping between us, ji,' she told me in a flat voice. 'His palm was turned upwards and it filled up with his father's blood.'

I almost gagged, but her calm, unhurried voice showed no change in tone.

We lapsed into a silence once more. And then, the gong that sounds the hours in the jail rang over our heads. It marked each hour, whether day or night, and startled sleeping bodies awake to remember and relive their past in images: a whirring ceiling fan spattered with blood or a child's innocent fist cupping the blood of his murdered father.

It was time for Janaki to leave. She stood up and folded her hands.

'Do you read the Ramayana, Janaki?' I asked.

'Yes,' she replied, her eyes hidden beneath her lashes once more.

Then one day, I thought to myself, she will come across these lines:

Pativanchak parpati rati karai
Raurav narak kalp shat parayi.

A woman who cheats on her husband
Goes to that most terrible hell – Raurav

'Can I leave now, ji?' she repeated.

'I nodded and tried to smile but could not frame my lips around one. I watched her retreating back, held upright, and thought: there is an eighteen-year-old girl still trapped inside that frame. Is she still alive or has she been snuffed out forever before she could bloom? Or had nature taught her to repeat the lines we used to teach our parrots in our childhood:

Sundari tain sooli bhali
Birla bache koi
Loh nihala agni main
Jali bali koyla hoi . . .

Fear a beautiful woman more than the noose
Even the flames of a fire cannot destroy her power

A Village of the Dead

When I was first introduced to the village of corpses I was a mere child. Perhaps that is why the impression it made on my mind is as firm as a footprint on wet cement and I remember every detail so vividly.

My father was then the home minister to the Maharaja of Orchcha and looked after the state jail. He had introduced several improvements in the condition of the lives of criminals and it was at his initiative that those accused of murder were freed of wearing a ball and chain on their feet. One such prisoner used to come every day to our house to work in the garden. For eighteen years, he had carried the iron ball in his hands as he moved, one step at a time, so even after he was freed of that burden, his feet moved slowly. Two deep gashes ran round his ankles and had become bleeding sores.

'What was your crime, bandi?' I asked him one day. He looked at me, his fearsome moustache bristling, and replied matter-of-factly: 'I cut off my sahib's neck, binnoo!'

'Why?' I went on, and he was silent. Perhaps he was trying to figure out how he could summarize his crime to suit a child's understanding. Bansi had killed his firangi boss, and yet, managed to escape the death penalty. Perhaps the judge felt that, in a curious way, he was a victim of his circumstances. After all, his boss was guilty of a terrible crime against Bansi. He had snatched his khansama's wife and made her his mistress. Had his wife not managed to escape Bansi's fury, her head would have rolled on the ground as well. Whatever the reason, Bansi's death sentence had been commuted to life imprisonment.

Bansi was the headman of 'the village of corpses' – a euphemism for the inmates of the jail. Once, he took a truck full of 'villagers' to the temple at Kundeswar; my father had been responsible for granting him permission to do that. The joy on their faces at seeing the glorious sky overhead, clearly visible from our terrace next door to the temple, is a sight I can never forget. My father had a huge vessel of jalebis sent over for them and their shouts of joy and full-throated hurrahs for my father rent the sky.

Years later, I was in the vicinity again and went once again to visit the village of corpses. This time, my brother was the private secretary to the maharaja of Orchcha. The old warden of the jail was still around and I persuaded my brother to let me accompany him to the jail one day. At first, he was horrified by my request. 'How can you even think of such an absurd thing?' he asked. 'Girls from good families don't go near a jail!' However, when his new bride, my sister-in-law, added her shy voice to mine, he had to give in. We reached the outer precincts and were a little thrown by the sheer size of the thick walls that seemed to tower over the area. Just two intimidating syllables were painted in bold letters over the arch that led in: 'Jail'. How different those jails were from the ones you see now!

The state jailor had a personality to suit his job: he wore tight khaki Jodhpurs, carried a whip in his hand and had a well-waxed moustache. That moustache alone carried more authority than a posse of policemen. Like the flowers around the necks of the gods that are said never to wither, I am sure the moustache of a jailor remains black, bushy and frightening even after he retires. One roar from him had people trembling and not one prisoner had the temerity to lift his eyes when he strode into a cell. He took us on a guided tour of the jail and then to the smithy, where the prisoners themselves fashioned the balls and chains they were forced to wear. He proudly displayed handcuffs they had made, asking us to weigh a pair in our hands. I realized that this was a ploy to distract us from asking him to take us to meet the prisoners, among them a notorious dacoit of Madhya Pradesh, Deshpat. His Robin Hood-like exploits had become legend and lore by then: how he looted a village or burgled the house of a famous Seth in Lalitpur within minutes, then donated the loot to the family of a poor girl so that they could marry her off . . .

'Come, I'll take you all to meet Deshpat,' the jailor said finally, and my sister-in-law and I began to tremble at the prospect of meeting the legendary daku. I couldn't believe that we would finally meet the Deshpat who had inspired ballads in the neighbouring villages of Bundelkhand. When he was brought in, he stood there with folded hands, a lithe body, salt and pepper hair and a face full of deep lines. His eyes were as calm and deep as the surface of a quiet lake. He bent low over our feet and then stood up. My eyes filled up – it was like watching a bird caught in a cage. How it must hurt this proud man to bend before two young girls, I thought. We sat in awkward silence, then he turned politely to the jailor and asked, 'Can I go now, sarkar? It is almost time for the prisoners' lunch.'

'Deshpat oversees the prison meals,' the jailor explained to us. 'So, what have you made today, Deshpat?'

He laughed and his two missing front teeth lent his face a curious youthfulness as he threw back his head. 'What else but the same old chane ki daal and roti, sarkar?'

'Go, fetch some on a clean plate for these girls,' the jailor ordered him. 'Let's see what you think of their food,' he said to us. A short while later, Deshpat arrived, holding a plate with our food. Two fat chapatis and a small bowl of chane ki daal rested neatly on it and next to them was the special tomato chutney he had made just for us by roasting tomatoes on a griddle and squashing the pulp with some chillies and salt. It tasted delicious and, in no time, we had gobbled up the lot. The taste of that meal still sits on my tongue as a tantalizing memory. After meeting Deshpat, I thought I could go another step, so I placed my next request before the jailor. 'Please take us to the death row,' I begged him.

'No, no!' He almost threw up his hands in horror. 'I can't take you there. Those men are wild, they speak the kind of vile language that ears such as yours should never have to hear. And if your mother hears I took you there, she'll kill me.' He began to herd us out, but I dug my heels in. Finally, he agreed to take us.

We crossed the huge courtyard and went to the far end of the jail. The low roofs and tiny cells shocked me: how could a grown man live here? There were just two prisoners there and, one day, at an appropriate signal from the jailor, they would be led to their death. The state hangman had a practised wrist – he knew exactly how to grease a noose so that it slid over their heads and killed them with a single flick. Heavy beards covered the faces of the two men who stood clutching the iron bars of their cells. They yelled some obscene words at us, but before they could say more, the jailor quickly led us away.

Nearby was the lone woman prisoner on the death row. A maalin, she was due to be hanged in a month's time. She had a veil drawn over her face and had vowed to never lift it, we were told. She wanted no one to see her face and had declared that she would not even unveil her face at the time of her hanging. 'How can I face girls from good families, sarkar?' she told the jailor when we asked to see her face.

How times have changed since then! Now, when after all these years, I went to interview some prisoners in the women's jail in Lucknow, they had no such qualms. Like blasé strippers, they narrated their stories to me without any visible hesitation, hardly faltering even when they came to the goriest details. My pen froze occasionally, but not their tongues. Their exposure to the relentless interrogation by the police, the press and the court had made them clinical about themselves and their crime – they were like actors who read their parts mechanically before an audience. Each had a story that was fit for dramatization, and each provided my pen with new material.

I was presented with fresh drama each time I went there. This time, it was a tall, dark woman who refused to meet my eyes. I felt as if I had seen her somewhere, but I could not place her face. Then it dawned on me that she was like one of the dark women of the artist B. Prabha's works – the same sadness and the same fleshy lips that are the hallmarks of her portraits. Yet, when she came and sat down next to me and I studied her face closely, I realized that the innocence of B. Prabha's models was missing here – this one was like a fruit that had been artificially ripened, and so her face had none of the natural sweetness of Prabha's village belles.

I had been told that she was the moll of a famous dacoit whose name spelt terror. Then one day, he was caught and his gang rounded up. Now, he was languishing in a jail in Delhi and his wife was here, many miles away in Lucknow. There were just two months left of her sentence and I wondered what she would do after she was free. Apparently, she had stashed away 120 tolas of gold in a bank in Kanpur, which she claimed was her dowry, not looted goods.

Each time the gang came back after a looting spree, they would give her gold and jewellery. She would then melt it down and stash it away to be made into some other piece later. Her husband, occasionally oppressed with the loneliness of the life he had chosen, would whisk her away to some town to savour the bright life. A car would wait for them in a dark alley and she would accompany her husband, dressed in her fine jewels, to go on a spree to Bareilly, Lucknow or Kanpur.

'Did you never feel guilt about accepting the stolen goods your husband placed at your feet?' I asked.

'No,' she replied glibly. 'How was I to know that he got them after looting or killing someone?' She looked up at my face; something in it must have made her pause, for suddenly the mask slipped. There had been no stopping Janaki once she started to tell me her story, but this one was like a vicious snake: she emerged from her basket to hiss at me when provoked, then slipped into her basket once more.

'So why are you here?' I nudged her again.

'For aiding and abetting in crime: my husband is accused of seven dacoities and murder,' she answered in a low voice, avoiding my eyes. We played this cat-and-mouse game until I managed to get the story out of her.

Her husband returned one day from one of his secret ventures to find her upset and depressed. A lonely life in a forest was hardly conducive to making a person happy, and then the unending flights to new hiding places, the eternal wait for a husband who may never return. She could trust no one, nor confide in a friend. Who knew when a member of the gang may decide to sell his mates to the police for a few coins? That day, when he returned, he threw a bundle at her feet. Wrapped in dirty rags, it was a king's ransom in precious stones and jewellery such as she had never seen. She took one necklace from the lot and, with trembling hands, placed it around her neck and for a moment she tried to forget the neck that had probably been hacked off to snatch this treasure. 'Wear it today,' her husband told her. 'But I know they will come after me for this: tomorrow we will have to melt it down.'

'Never,' she replied. 'Melt this exquisite thing? I'll hide it in my clothes, no one will know.'

The vanity of a woman often makes her reckless – until she can hear someone exclaim over a piece of jewellery and sigh in envy, what is a necklace worth?

'We were returning from Bareilly after a late-night movie,' she recalled in a sad voice and my nerves started tingling at the tone of her voice. I could almost picture the scene – a stolen car, she and her husband wearing shiny new clothes, cheap scent, a new purse on her lap, her husband's mouth savouring a paan and the sleepy aftermath of a late-night show. The driver was speeding when he felt they were being followed.

'Looks like the police are behind us,' the driver said over his shoulder. His hands were trembling by now and the car zigzagged dangerously as he tried to speed away. 'Didn't I tell you not to wear that wretched necklace?' her husband snarled in anger. 'If we are caught with that thing round your neck, we're done for.'

She quickly took off the stolen goods and hid some in her purse and some inside her clothes, but to no avail. The police took little time to unearth them and the owner identified them as stolen goods. That is how she had landed here, she said. Today, there were two letters for her from her husband and the postcards, kept on a nearby table, were easy to read. I blushed as I read the few sentences that I managed to see.

The interview over, she stood with folded hands and prepared to leave.

As she turned, I couldn't help asking: 'You will be free soon. What do you plan to do after that?'

She stared at me for a few minutes as if I were a policeman interrogating her before parole, and then said: 'Work as a teacher somewhere. I've passed the eighth class here and will try and get a job.'

I wonder, though, how far that will work out. Having got accustomed to the free life of the forest, the power of the moll will not be easy to give up or forget. Where will she find gold to cook, I wonder, or savour the delicious curry made from a fresh kill? Enjoy the the stealthy outings made in a stolen car, the money-filled purse on her lap and the jewellery worth a king's ransom worth that she was used to wearing?

Muggi

My reverie was broken when the doctor entered and asked: 'Shall I send the next one in?' I nodded, unable to speak to a normal person so soon after an exposure to someone's abnormal life. I had been told the next person was the clown of the jail – and my heart lifted a little at the prospect of meeting this one. It was like yearning for a spoon of sugar after swallowing a bitter dose of castor oil. So far, the ones I had met were like the practised trapeze artistes of a circus. They flirted with death as they swung dangerously from high tension ropes, trusting their life to another person's machinations. The clown was led in: a blank, foolish face, large expressionless eyes and a meaningless grin on her face.

'Here she is.' The doctor smiled as she brought her to where I sat. 'She goes home tomorrow. Listen, Muggi, I just got a letter from your husband – he is looking forward to your return but is terrified of one thing . . .'

'What is that, memsahib?' She looked disturbed for a moment.

Naturally, he would be worried, I privately thought. Who would not be, faced with prospect of welcoming a wife who had been locked away for fourteen years?

The doctor smiled. 'He says' – she twinkled at Muggi – 'that he is worried you won't leave a single brick standing in his house.'

'No, no, sarkar!' Muggi's grin was back immediately on her foolish face and she touched her earlobes in horror. 'I won't eat them.'

I must have looked stunned at this exchange, so the doctor turned to me as she explained. 'This is a true child of the earth, Shivaniji,' she said. 'She has a thing about mud: give her a sakora or a kulhar, a flowerpot – anything made of mud – and she eats it up.' Muggi blushed and looked down at her toes.

No wonder she looked like a flowerpot herself, I thought. A dark swarthy face, a sari tied inches above her ankles and a kurti she seemed to be bursting out of. If she sneezed, the buttons would fly, I thought. She had no trace of womanly softness in her at all: her eyes, her walk, her face were singularly lacking in any grace. She sat in front of me, swinging her knees in a way that no decent woman would. And yet, she was capable of loving a man deeply. She blushed at his mention and her face registered the glow of a woman in love each time his name cropped up.

What a strange tale hers was! She was just fifteen years old when her sister's husband introduced her to a life that landed her here. At fifteen, Muggi exuded an animal sexuality that was unmistakeable and her swarthy skin fairly glowed with her youthful energy. She was initiated into the craft of charming gullible men and soon she became adept at that trade. Her body filled out and her fleshy lips and large eyes acquired the sly, animal cunning of a vixen. Her brother-in-law would find some grieving widower, eager to find a second wife to look after him and his children, and offer Muggi as a candidate. A quick wedding was organized and the two sisters would put up the drama of weeping and wailing when it was time for Muggi to leave for her new home. The poor groom was taken in completely as he tenderly led his bride away.

Muggi would then work on his family, quickly ingratiating herself with the mother-in-law, and soon she knew where the family stashed its wealth. Then one day, when the time was ripe, she decamped with everything, and neither she nor her brother-in-law could ever be traced. They would flee to another town and start their business under a new name, a new address. In twenty years, Muggi had conned fourteen husbands.

And then, Muggi fell in love.

I was reminded of Somerset Maugham's unforgettable short story 'Round Dozen'. The only difference was that in Maugham's story the confidence-trickster was a man, and this was a woman. Muggi's fifteenth husband was a blacksmith and Muggi was seduced by his vigorous lovemaking. She loved his glistening body to distraction. Often, she toyed with the idea of confessing everything to him: she would tell him, she thought, how she was innocently seduced by her own brother-in-law and sister into this life and now she wanted to reform herself. But suppose, she thought immediately, that he turned away from her in disgust? And so she would keep silent. Most men cannot tolerate even one other man in their wife's life – here she was with a cast of fourteen husbands behind her! Even Draupadi in the Mahabharata could not equal her record. And then, there was another problem. Her husband's mother was a devi – she loved Muggi like a daughter and Muggi, motherless herself, was overwhelmed by the love she found in this house. Muggi gave back to her husband's mother all the love she got from her. She worked tirelessly in the kitchen, oiled the old woman's hair religiously and combed it lovingly, rubbed her feet to ease her corns and even picked the lice from the old woman's hair.

Muggi's penchant for eating mud was a joke between them and whenever she saw Muggi looking pensive, the old woman would break a terracotta sakora in two and give it to her daughter-in-law, saying kindly: 'Here, Bahu, go on and eat it.' And she would tell the neighbours, 'Look at her! Any other bahu would crave sweets and savouries – all this one wants is a bit of earth!'

This earthen idyll was soon to be shattered. Her brother-in-law and sister began to get restive. It had never taken their student so long to accomplish her mission. What if their golden goose had been kidnapped by another player? And so her brother-in-law decided to go and check out matters for himself. He arrived at Muggi's house ostensibly to ask after her welfare and to complain that, even after six months, she had not visited her sister once. But the blacksmith was no fool and he was found out. Then started a sensational case that went on and on and fresh skeletons tumbled out of Muggi's past. Both she and her brother-in-law were convicted on charges of cheating and sent to jail. Muggi was given a lighter sentence and the day I met her was her last in the jail. She looked thrilled at the prospect of returning to her blacksmith and his mother.

'But will they accept her as willingly?' I asked the doctor. 'After all, they must know all about her past.'

'Her mother-in-law can't wait to welcome her daughter-in-law back,' she told me. 'Isn't that true, Muggi?' The doctor turned to Muggi as she said this to me. Perhaps her simple, uncomplicated nature had something in it after all, for Muggi blushed and looked down bashfully.

'Why don't you say something?' the doctor goaded her. But Muggi's face ducked even deeper into her chest. 'Do you know,' the doctor turned to me again, 'her mother-in-law visited her regularly in jail and never once forgot to bring her diyas and sakoras to eat.'

Muggi stuffed her pallu into her mouth as she giggled. 'I promise I won't eat another one all my life,' she said. The happiness on her face, suffused with the joy of returning to her husband and home, was infectious and both the doctor and I burst out laughing. As I got up to leave the cursed prison, I wanted to whisper in Muggi's ears, 'Go ahead and eat all the mud you want, Muggi!'

Any woman who can retain her sense of humour and her innocence after a prison sentence deserves all the happiness she gets. I silently blessed her as I left: 'May your mother-in-law keep feeding you bits of terracotta, may your blacksmith love you with all his heart, and may you find the happiness in your fifteenth marriage that was lacking in all the previous fourteen, Muggi. Amen!'

Alakh Mai and Rajula

As I bade goodbye to these unfortunate prisoners, two faces from my past seemed to accost me and ask: 'Why haven't you written about us? You met us long before you met these women.' I can see them as they stand before me: the middle-aged Vaishnavi, her hand rattling a long iron chimta, and next to her, the emaciated Rajula, a begging bowl in her hand and a nose-ring shining on her pale face.

How could I forget them? They were prisoners of a different order. No chains on their feet, no walls to crowd them in. They had the world under their feet and the wide open sky above their heads. They could roam wherever they wished, carrying their past locked in their hearts. No police or law officer ever dogged their steps: their bodies were free – but what about their souls?

This is the story of a nun, a Vaishnavi, who roamed from place to place – Badrinath, Kedarnath, Banaras, Haridwar – calling, '*Alakh mai, bhiksha de!*' In those days, you often came across such mendicants and I can recall several from my childhood who wore long ropes of rudraksha round their necks and came to seek alms at our door in Almora. No householder ever turned them away. Perhaps people were more generous (or god-fearing) in my childhood. Every Saturday and Tuesday, two Nepali Vaishnavis came to our house, calling '*Alakh mai, bhiksha de*!' Our cook would give them a large helping of rice and lentils in their bowl. Then they would leave, but not before showering blessings on me: 'May you grow up to marry a prince, Lalli. May you bring many brothers to this house: not one or two, but seven tall and strapping ones!'

How times have changed! Today, would any house consider a crop of seven sons a blessing? No wonder I often hear harsh voices shoo away mendicants: 'Why can't you work? There is nothing wrong with you – get out! I don't give alms to idlers!' However, I still can't turn away such people when I meet them, for my ears remember that sweet voice blessing me: 'May you grow up to marry a prince, Lalli. May you bring many brothers to this house: not one or two, but seven tall and strapping ones!'

Then one day, a completely new and deep voice called out: '*Alakh mai, bhiksha de!*' I peeped out, and there was a new Vaishnavi standing in the courtyard. Tall and broad, with a small ochre bag slung on her shoulder, she was rattling a long pair of tongs in her hands. What arrested my attention was her size and appearance: she looked a man in drag! She stood there imperiously, looking around her for some human contact and finding none, called out:

'Alakh Niranjan! Mai will eat here today.' Interestingly, she used the masculine gender when talking of herself, and I wondered if she were a woman at all. With her cropped hair she looked like a man, she spoke like one and certainly had the voice of one. Her broad chest showed no sign of womanly breasts and she was taller than any woman I had ever seen. Her flat nose had wide, flared nostrils that looked as if any minute now she would blow smoke out of them like a dragon!

She looked up and spotted me peering from behind a pillar on the veranda above the courtyard. 'You there, little girl,' she called to me. 'Did you hear me? Mai will eat here today, this is Guru's wish. Go, tell someone inside.' Then she planted her tongs in a flower bed and settled down to wait.

I was terrified. We siblings lived alone with our grandfather and had long finished our morning meal. Our cook, a forbidding Brahmin whom we called Lohaniji, had locked up the kitchen and was probably sleeping in his quarter. Where at this hour would I find food for this dragon?

'Mai, why don't you rest here?' I said politely. 'We have finished eating, but let me ask my sister if she can get some bhiksha for you.'

'No!' she thundered and rattled her tongs noisily. 'I told you I shall eat here today. Go get me some firewood and pots and some besan, curd and chillies. Mai will eat karhi-chawal today. Go!'

I was beginning to get a little irritated, but there was an

air of such authority about her that I found myself asking my sister to come and help me look for the ingredients for Mai's meal. By the time we reached the courtyard, Mai had once more planted her tongs close by and spread out her huge legs to make herself comfortable under our walnut tree.

'Come, children,' she greeted us. 'Have you brought what I asked for?' She leant her bulk against the tree and squinted at us. We put down the lot before her; within minutes, she had erected a makeshift stove with two stones, lit a fire and put a pot of karhi on it to cook. Then she began cleaning the rice and turned to us again.

'Alakh Guru! Do you want to ask anything? Mai does not come here often. She has come today because Guruji sent her.'

At first, we couldn't understand what she meant, then she took a handful of rice grains and shut her eyes, mumbling some incomprehensible mantra. Both of us were thoroughly scared by now: who was this woman? A witch?

'What do you want to know? Something about the one you will marry?' She focused her red eyes on us – they were glowing like coals.

'I have decided never to marry,' my sister said smugly. 'So I don't need to ask you anything about my future husband.' This was true: she had declared her decision quite firmly to our family a while ago and I think they had accepted it. But, obviously, Mai knew something else. 'You will marry,' she told my sister firmly. 'No power on earth will ever stop that from happening.' She said this with such conviction that I could almost hear the sound of a band and a wedding procession outside our gates.

Then she broke the spell by turning her attention to her cooking and adopted a completely different tone as she started to chat with us. I watched her as she fiddled with the pots and pans. Not only did she look like a man, she even had a faint moustache on her upper lip. For a moment, the same thought flashed through our heads: was this some wicked man who had come disguised as a woman to kidnap us? As if she could read our thoughts, Mai flashed her teeth at us. 'Scared you, did I?' she said and suddenly grasped my hand. A shiver of pure horror ran through me: I felt as if a huge, slimy lizard had fallen on my hand. I still cannot describe what her touch was like without shuddering at the memory.

'Don't be put off by my face, child,' she said kindly. She sighed deeply as she ran a hand over her moustache. 'My name was Laxmi, and when I came to my husband's house as a bride, my mother-in-law took one look at me and said to her son, "This is not a Laxmi, my son – this looks like a Laxman Singh." She and I became mortal enemies from that day on.' Her deep voice began to sound gruff now, as if she had a bad cold. Our eyes went to the beads around her neck and she introduced each one to us. 'This was given by the big Guru Maharaj when he accepted me as his disciple. This one, by the next guru for saying my prayers, and this one came from a cremation ground. These tulsi beads I picked up when I went for the Kumbh to Prayag.'

My sister got up then, signalling to me to go inside as

well, but I was so enchanted by the stories the Vaishnavi told that I pretended I hadn't felt her nudge. The Vaishnavi did not notice this sideshow as her attention was on her food. She first prepared three little morsels for her gurus and then turned to me. 'Want some?'

To tell you the truth, I was tempted by the sight of that spicy karhi, but how could I possibly eat the alms I had given? I shook my head.

She finished her meal and scrubbed the pots and pans till they glistened, then picked a few embers from the dying fire to light her chillum. She foraged in her shoulder bag for a small red box and snorted some snuff into her huge nostrils. Then she took a deep puff of her chillum and really turned into a dragon with smoke coming out of her nostrils.

'Vah!' she declared in a satisfied tone. 'Mai is very happy with you today, child.' I was fascinated by the size of her palm and tried to imagine what a slap from her would mean. Was she a Vaishnavi or a wrestler?

'Do you really walk all day and night, Mai?' I asked

Her bloodshot eyes considered my question indulgently.

'Yes, child. Mai committed a terrible crime once. This is why God has cursed her to walk day and night and never rest. She plants these tongs wherever her guru commands her to, and when she hears his voice she picks them up, says "Alakh" and sets off again. Snowstorms, thunderstorms, raging torrents and streams – she has survived them all. She has sinned, child, so this is now her fate. She does whatever her guru tells her to, whatever he tells her . . .'

She touched her hands reverently to her forehead at the mention of her guru, then took a long puff from her chillum and floated off into a trance.

Guru? Where was he? What kind of guru was this, whom she could hear yet I could not see? Was he a magician who whispered his command into her ears and then vanished?

'Ha, ha, ha!' The Vaishnavi roared with laughter. 'Silly child, how can you see Guru Maharaj? He comes silently like a breeze and whispers in Mai's ears alone. He stays with Mai all the time, child. Day and night, wherever she goes, he goes with her and tells her not to be afraid – wherever she goes, whether the cremation ground, or the burning ghats.'

If she visited burning ghats and cremation grounds, how could she be a Vaishnavi, I wondered. Was she some tantrik's disciple? The hair on my neck rose as I remembered something that had happened recently in our neighbourhood. A Vaishnavi came one day to these neighbours' house, planted her tongs in their courtyard and established herself there. The simple housewife allowed to her stay on. There were rumours that the Vaishnavi offered meat and alcohol when she did her puja and brought terrible times to the host's family. First, they lost their newborn son, then the head of the family died and, finally, the lady of the house lost her mind. Then, as mysteriously as she had come, the Vaishnavi disappeared one day. I began to tremble as I wondered whether this Vaishnavi was someone like that.

With her eyes still closed, my Vaishnavi began to speak in a low voice.

'Mai was ten years old when she got married and was sent to her husband's home after four years. His name was Aan Singh and he ran a flourishing transport company. His lorries ran all over the *terai* – Tanakpur, Haldwani and Almora. Half the petrol went into the lorries, the other half into his belly. Used to come back drunk, and then mother and son took turns to thrash Mai. Go fetch some wood, they would tell her. Or, go to the jungle and cut a bundle of grass for the animals at home. Often, they sent her to graze the buffalo in the jungle. No one ever fed her a morsel or gave her even a sip of water. That bloody buffalo was another evil spirit – it would make poor Mai run all over the jungle and exhaust her. If Mai ever asked her mother-in-law, can I visit my mother, the witch would brand her with hot tongs for her request.'

At this point, Mai propped her chillum against the tree and rolled up her clothes. Her torso was an ugly mass of weals, proof of the abuse she had suffered in her husband's home. So she *was* a woman, I realized as I glanced furtively at her wasted breasts.

'One day, when Mai was burning with fever, her mother-in-law ordered her to take the buffalo for grazing to the jungle.' She continued her story. 'Mai wept and pleaded, told her there was a leopard in the jungle too, and she said: "Good! If it eats you up, we'll get a proper daughter-in-law for this house."'

It seemed the wretched buffalo had been primed to

torture Mai by the old hag: it was so frisky that day that Mai was run off her feet. Finally, the creature stood grazing at the edge of a ravine that rose in a sheer precipice from the raging waters of the Kali Ganga in the valley. If anyone toppled over, not even a fragment of bone would survive. Mai was really angry that day – angry at her hunger, angry at the old hag, angry at her drunkard husband – and decided to take it all out on that buffalo. She gave it one heave – and down it plunged, sailing over the precipice like a blade of grass.

Then Mai went home weeping, and the old hag asked: 'What happened? Where is the buffalo, you wretch?'

'In the jungle, saas-jyu. Come I'll show you,' said Mai.

Her cursing, screaming mother-in-law followed Mai to the jungle, to the same ravine. The old woman was a thin, fragile creature and Mai a strapping young woman . . .

'Where is my precious buffalo?' the hag screeched.

'There,' said Mai, and pushed the old woman over the edge.

'She went like a blade of grass, child, like a blade of grass . . .'

When Mai reached home, a furious Aan Singh was waiting for her with an axe in his hands, drunk out of his mind, his eyes burning like coals. 'Where were you, whore?' he yelled. 'How dare you come home alone? When you know a leopard roams that jungle, how dare you take my mother there?'

Mai was livid: the bastard could think of his mother and his wretched buffalo – had he ever spared a thought for Mai?

'Your mother fell down a gorge,' Mai wailed. 'Come quickly with me, she is hanging from a tree, we may be able to rescue her yet . . .'

Aan Singh ran to the spot. He swiped a blow across Mai's cheek, saying, 'What have you done to my mother? Where is she, you whore?'

'There,' said Mai, and shoved him down the sharp precipice to the raging Kali Ganga below.

'Mai never returned home after that, child, never.'

She went to a cave where a Nepali guru maharaj lived, fell at his feet and confessed her crimes. Guru Maharaj accepted her as his disciple and said, 'Go, Mai, from now on roam the land and eat and wear what others give you. This is the penance you must perform for what you have done. From now on, remember, God alone will look after you, He is your only support . . .'

The Vaishanvi picked up her tongs and bag, dusted herself and stood up laughing. 'God bless you, child, Mai has to leave now . . .'

Before I could say anything or call my sister, she had descended the steps of the courtyard and vanished.

I used this masculine Vaishnavi as a character in two stories: 'Lati' and 'Dhuan'. Later, she made a sort of guest appearance in my novel *Chaudah Phere*. Her extraordinary story continues to haunt me till today. In one day, this woman had snuffed out not one but three lives – a buffalo, a mother-in-law and a husband. And yet, can anyone deny that she had a reason? No court heard of this triple murder, no lawmaker pronounced judgment on her and no jailor kept her in prison. She became her own jailor, the chains on her feet clamped there by her own conscience. What also caught my attention was the fourth murder she committed but never spoke of: when she stood at the edge of the precipice and decided to hurl her youth, her desires and aspirations, forever into the raging torrents of the Kali Ganga. They floated down that ravine like a blade of grass and left a celibate Vaishnavi where a young girl once stood. Did any law court ever pronounce a more terrible punishment?

At this point, another prisoner of conscience stands before my eyes. I first met Rajula under the same walnut tree under which the Vaishnavi had planted her tongs. Rajula carried a small tambourine in her hand and sang the *Riturain* songs of spring in a high, sweet voice. In the Almora of my childhood, bands of professional folk singers would arrive in the month of March, at the start of spring, and go from one prominent home to another to entertain people with the traditional folk songs of the season at *Chaitra baithaks*, or private spring concerts. Unlike professional singing girls, there was no trace of the bazaar about these women. They wore velvet ghaghras trimmed with lace and their faces were discreetly veiled with odhnis. Their tinkling laughter rang through dull courtyards and lit up the lives of the stern Brahmin havelis.

Another, rather less attractive, tradition of those days also comes to my mind. Several older men from the highborn Brahmin families in Kumaon had installed a singing girl as a mistress in their homes. A 'Ram' was prefixed to the name of the singing girl to make it socially acceptable, so it was quite possible to meet a Ramkatori, Rampriya or Rampyari at an uncle's house. Naturally, the most lively Chaitra baithaks were organized in homes where one of their own lived as the mistress of the householder. Unfortunately, no one in our neighbourhood had such a patroness, but that did not stop us from running to the windows whenever we heard a band of singers singing their way to a baithak.

One day, I went across to a neighbouring relative's house to borrow their newspaper. I barged into my great-uncle's private sitting area – and I will never forget what I saw. My great-uncle, cigar in hand, was reclining on a bolster, surrounded by giggling apsaras. My eyes were dazzled by the colours of their bright clothes and the scent of their bodies. It seemed as if someone had sprinkled a dozen bottles of perfume in the room. For a moment, the old man was nonplussed at the sight of his great-niece, but he recovered his composure quickly. With remarkable aplomb, considering his posture and surroundings, he asked me kindly, 'What brings you here, child?'

'I wanted to borrow the *Statesman*,' I stammered.

'Oh, is this your granddaughter, Lalla? We must sing the first song of Chaitra for her, then.' One of the apsaras smiled. And before my great-uncle or I could say anything, I was surrounded, like a queen bee by her worker bees, by their honey-sweet voices:

May this auspicious day
Come a thousand times
In the lives of our daughters . . .

I was touched, caressed and smothered by those hands and voices. Unused to such loving touches on my body, I was nearly reduced to tears of embarrassment. Sensing my discomfiture, my great-uncle said sharply: 'What is all this? Go, child.' Then his voice gentled. 'The paper is lying there. Pick it up and take it home.'

The old man was a widower, and childless to boot. Perhaps his mistress, longing for a child to fuss over, was responsible for that episode. Years later, Maupassant's 'Madame Tellier's Establishment' reminded me strongly of that day. Maupassant's story is about the madame of a brothel, Madame Tellier, who takes her lively, giggling band of prostitutes to attend a niece's baptism. He describes brilliantly the havoc that ensues in the Catholic home of her brother as this exotic band of Parisian butterflies descends on a simple village.

My ears still ring with the sweet *Riturain* song set to *Raga Desh* that they sang for me that day.

May this auspicious day
Come a thousand times
In the lives of our daughters . . .

So when Rajula came with her tambourine to our courtyard, singing the same song, I was stunned. She was dark and her eyes were deep pools of sadness. Her sweet voice had an attractive break and a nasal twang, like the poignant wail of a shehṇai. I now realize that she was probably syphilitic, for her nose had collapsed, and that was probably why her voice had that nasal quality.

'What shall I sing for you, Lalli?' she asked me. '*Riturain*, *Pari Chanchari* or *Ramola* . . .?'

She came almost every day and her fund of folk songs had all of us eating out of her hands. She generously shared her treasure trove with me and I eagerly learnt as many as I could to take back to Santiniketan. Kanika Devi, Jyotishdev Burman, Suchitra Mitra were my contemporaries, and we often used these lovely pahari tunes in our impromptu concerts. *Tilak Kamod*, *Desh* and *Durga* – these were the three ragas that gave life to the folk songs of Kumaon. Rajula had learnt them from her mother and given them a flavour all her own. She was born to sing, and when I hear the Malwa folk songs that Kumar Gandharva sings, I remember her artless and un-self-conscious singing with new respect. She would take a note to the highest pitch and leave it there to float in silence – then, after a pause, she would pick it up from the base and play with it as if the song was a kite.

She had no accompaniments, just a small, battered tambourine. Often, she lit a flame to warm its sagging skin and bring it to life. Then, she would shut her eyes, place a hand on her ear and sing. When she sang '*Beru pako bara masa* . . .' – that famous Kumaoni folk song that everyone has heard – I swear that even the walnuts on our tree turned red with passion.

'Rajula, where did you learn to sing like this?' I asked her once.

'From Him.' She closed her eyes and pointed heavenwards.

No human being could have given her that voice – so

Rajula was right, her voice had to be a divine gift. She sang all the *Riturain* songs – *Bhagnaula, Ramola*, the lot – but when she sang a hymn called '*Kariye Chhima*' ('Forgive me'), she was at her best.

What I have said, or left unsaid
What I heard, or did not hear
What I did, or left undone
Forgive me for all that, my Lord

She would go into a trance, her eyes streaming with tears as she asked Him for forgiveness. I have seen her move her audience to tears when she sang her special song.

'Why do you have to beg when you have such a voice, Rajula?' I asked once. By now, she and I had a special bond that grew from our shared love of music. Rajula became silent.

'Don't ask, Lalli. By the grace of people such as yourself, Rajula earned so much that she could have built ten such palaces for herself by now,' she replied, pointing to our haveli. For a moment, something like pride lit up the pools of darkness in her eyes.

'So?' I prompted her. 'Where did all that money go?'

'Into the river,' she said and dropped the tambourine into her lap.

'Don't joke, Rajula.' I held her hands as I begged her for an explanation. 'Tell me where that money went.'

'What is the use of that, Lalli?' she asked sadly. 'You come from a highborn Brahmin home, Lalli, your touch can wash away the sins of a fallen woman like me. You are my gangajal, Lalli. I cannot hold your hand and lie. I threw away forty tolas of gold . . .'

'Forty *tolas* of gold?' I gasped.

'Yes, Lalli,' she said, nodding tonelessly.

'Not just that,' she went on. 'Four thousand silver coins with Victoria's face on them, I threw those into the Bhagirathi as well.'

'But why did you do such an insane thing, Rajula? You have to beg for your food now . . . Why, when you had so much, did you . . .?'

'There was a reason, Lalli, I had sinned. Committed a heinous crime. I was just not caught, that's all. God must have shut His eyes that day,' she said and gave a wan smile. Then her pale face went paler still, and she muttered, 'I killed someone, Lalli.'

I held my breath.

'I killed my own son.'

I peered into her face, but her eyes were dry; perhaps she had used up all her tears.

'Why?' I whispered. 'Why did you do such a thing, Rajula?'

'Because he was the spitting image of his father, Lalli. When I could see his father's features in his face from the minute he was born, just imagine – what would happen when he grew up and went out in the world? Everyone would know whose child he was.' She took a deep breath and continued in a steady voice: 'So I took him to the river, shut my eyes and held him there until he drowned.'

What a strange woman this was! Most mothers would

consider it a badge of pride to give birth to a son who resembled his father – and here was Rajula, who had killed hers for the same reason!

'You won't understand, Lalli.' She answered my unspoken question as she patted me kindly. 'My whole village used to worship his father and, after all, I was not even his wedded wife. I was a lowly singing girl, God's handmaiden, the fallen woman of the village. How could I let his name be tarnished? I ran away from the village that night and dropped all my worldly goods in the Bhagirathi. Don't ask me what I have suffered and where I went after that, Lalli. May God forgive us all!' She touched her hands reverently to her forehead.

'God punished me for that crime: I lost my voice, dreadful sores broke out all over my body, Lalli. I was like a leper whom people shunned and moved away from. Occasionally, a kind soul would toss a few coins my way as I lay under a tree. And the nightmares!' She shuddered as she recalled them. 'I dreamt my clothes were drenched with the milk from my breasts, I wanted to scream but no sound came from my throat any more. Then, one day, I sang "*Kariye Chhima*", the song you love. And a miracle took place. My voice came back! The voice I had lost. Now I walk from home to home and sing "*Kariye Chhima*", Lalli. This is the penance God has decided I must perform, and I bow to His will.'

Rajula must have died by now, but her tambourine and the tinkle of her voice come back ever so often to me. Years later, Rajula became the heroine of my novella

Kariye Chhima, and I felt as if I had finally been able to repay the woman who taught me music more beautiful than I have ever heard.

Rajula and the Vaishnavi opened my eyes to a truth that I have grappled with ever since. That there is no jail on earth that can shackle a free spirit and no spirit so free that its feet cannot be bound in chains we cannot see.

PART TWO

Naseem

Sometimes, an unexpected encounter in a strange place brings you face to face with someone from the past. You know the face, but your wretched memory stubbornly refuses to come to your rescue. As soon as that person disappears, your memory awakes mischievously and you look frantically for the lost face, but by then it has disappeared once again. Chances are you will never meet that person again, for fate seldom smiles twice. And what you are left with is a deep sense of disquiet and regret.

Last month, something like this happened to me. She was there, right in front of me, but by the time I remembered who she was, she had vanished like an arrow in the surrounding darkness. I combed the length and breadth of the platform, but no, she was gone. Just a few moments ago, it seemed, she was here, sitting under the dim light of the railway waiting room, an untidy bundle next to her on the dirty floor . . .

But then, how could I have possibly imagined that I

would meet her like this? The last time I saw her, she was getting out of a car in our porch, wearing a lace-trimmed salwar and a red kurta. Her dupatta, glinting with the mica motes that had been added to the starch, glittered with each step she took. Behind her was her aunt, Bua Bi, and behind them followed a train of maids. One carried a huge paandan, another a basket of golden Malihabadi Dussehri mangoes for us and still another leapt to keep Bua Bi's dupatta from trailing in the dust. Every year, after their return from Lucknow, the aunt and niece would arrive at our house in Tikamgarh, laden with gifts for us. Apart from the delectable Dussehri mangoes, they brought us rose-scented rewris and iced fruit encased in balls of frozen water scented with kewra and aniseed. This last gift was what we loved the most – as soon as you dissolved the iced balls in a tumbler of water, it was transformed magically into fragrant sherbet. I think the artists who made these magic balls in Lucknow have vanished now – I've never seen them since Bua Bi's time.

To us children, Bua Bi was the epitome of elegance and beauty. She was plump but gorgeously so. I think voluptuous would be a better word to describe her. Her fair, round face glowed with love and her surma-darkened eyes were intoxicating pools of mystery. As children, we sat around her for hours, listening to her chaste Urdu and her wonderful stories. Once, when I was lying in bed with my eyes shut, nursing a toothache, my room was suddenly filled with a familiar fragrance. Bua Bi smiled at me gently when I opened my eyes and caressed my cheek with a soft palm. I felt as if a perfumed, silken handkerchief had been draped over my throbbing cheek and the pain almost vanished.

Perhaps their elegant Lucknow haveli is still around, its walls hung with glittering mirrors, sparkling white sheets, floor cushions, marble statues and a tinkling fountain decorating the house. What used to fascinate me most was a mysterious fragrant smoke that seemed to arise from an unseen source somewhere. Bua Bi was the favourite courtesan of the maharaja of Orchha, and they say that he was so moved by a dadra she once sang for him – '*Chale jaiyo bedarda, main roye chali jaaon . . .*' – that he gifted her with a jagir of her own. Bua Bi sang with a palm cupped over one ear, like the famous Rasoolan Bai, who along with such noted singers such as Siddheswari Devi, Kamla Jharia and Dulari would come to Tikamgarh to sing at state occasions. No one frowned at us if we accompanied the Tikamgarh princesses to meet these famous ladies. They taught us how to sit and rise gracefully, how to speak softly and even how to cut areca nuts stylishly. When Siddheswari Devi came for the crown prince's engagement, she taught us two classic ways of cutting: *bajra* and *motia*. Often, my readers ask me how I know so much about courtesans despite my strict Brahmin upbringing and I want to tell them that, in our innocent eyes, these women were not courtesans. They came to meet my mother as a beloved aunt would and that is what they were to us ever after.

When Naseem came with her khala to Tikamgarh for the first time, a small gold nose-ring dangled from her dainty nose. Her large eyes, outlined with dark surma, made her dark pupils fairly glow. When she smiled, two dimples appeared on her cheeks and stayed on even when the smile faded. 'I'll tell khala to bring me here more often,' she told me. 'I love your house.' She spent the whole day with us and would willingly have spent the night as well, but she was called away by her khala. Then, for two or three years, we never saw her. The fourth year, during a celebration at the fort, I bumped into her and we ran to embrace each other. It seemed to me that in the three years that we had not seen her, her khala had rubbed some magical potions on her – she was now voluptuously rounded and even more beautiful. At the Dussehra durbar that year, she sang a dadra that haunts me even today. In fact, when I hear it sung by another voice, I shut my eyes and Naseem floats in front of me, her legs folded neatly under her, singing:

Nathuniya ne, hai Rama, bara dukh deena!
Jab main ho gayi pandrah baras ki,
Godi main mohe dhar leena . . .

What trouble my gold nose-ring brought me!
As soon as I turned fifteen,
My lover pulled me onto his lap . . .

Her gold nose-ring had now been replaced by a sparkling diamond stud that shone proudly on her nose. Colourful glass bangles tinkled with each movement of her hands and she had everyone spellbound. She saw me in the audience and came over, her head covered with a dupatta, to embrace me warmly. 'Looks like you forgot all about your friend, Binnoo,' she chided me softly. 'You never sent me even one letter!'

'What about you?' I countered. 'Did you ever write to me?'

'How could I? I've never studied in a school, Binnoo, and even if I had asked someone to write it, it would have been in Urdu,' she said sadly. 'I didn't want that some third person should read what I wanted to write and tell you . . .'

'What did you want to keep secret, Naseem?' I asked innocently. 'And why have you taken off that lovely gold nose-ring? It looked so sweet on you!'

When I remember my foolish question now, I blush with shame. Her sad eyes filled up with tears and she brought down her eyelids to shutter them. Then, one afternoon, when there was no chaperone around, she told me the story of her deflowering. How she had committed the cardinal sin of falling in love with her royal lover and how she had worshipped him.

'He's told me he'll soon make me his bride and take me home,' she told me, blushing madly. 'I'll dress you in red, he says. You know, he is the grandson of a nawab sahib,' she boasted coyly. 'He's fair like a firangi and goes to an English madrasa.' Then, after a furtive look around the room, she dived into her bodice and pulled out a scented envelope that had her young swain's photograph. He looked a mere schoolboy, clad in his hockey shorts and shirt, swinging a hockey stick, smiling confidently into the camera.

'Careful, Naseem.' I laughed. 'He looks as if his amma will pull his ears any minute!'

'Rubbish!' she retorted angrily, stuffing the photograph back into its hiding place. 'He's not the kind to get bullied by his amma. Do you know how he bullies me around? You should see the way he lies on his bed and orders me to unlace his shoes!'

We talked for hours and she handed me the gifts she had brought from Lucknow. 'There are some lac bangles and some surma for you in this pouch,' she said as she handed it over. 'And here is my special present,' she added. 'A rainbow dupatta we call satrangi. I asked the dyer to add shamatulambar perfume to the starch so that you will never forget me when you smell it.'

Poor Naseem – is there any perfume in the world that stays forever? God knows where that rainbow satrangi is now, or where that shamatulambar scent and Naseem disappeared! All I have is one sad letter written by her, but because it was in Urdu, I had to seek the help of our durban, Chand Khan, to read it out to me.

'May I die if you don't write back to me immediately,' she had written. 'What is there left to write anyway? I am going off to Bihar because my aunt who lives in Ara has sent for me. I will probably set up shop there from now on . . .'

She sent me no address for her Bihar shop, nor did she ever write again. So when, after all these years, at twelve-thirty in the morning she came into the waiting room of a railway station in the middle of nowhere, and that too clad in a burqa, I had no idea that this was my Naseem. All she had with her was a bedding rolled in a coarse dhurrie and a battered aluminium tiffin carrier. She threw them carelessly in one corner and sprawled out in the only free armchair to sleep. The chowkidar came in muttering: 'Everyone thinks they can come and use the *phurst-kilass* waiting room for free! Bua' – he poked her rudely – 'do you have a ticket?'

'Arre, Beta, just let me rest my weary bones,' she whined. 'I'll leave in a little while. May Allah bless you, son, may He shower you with happiness.' The pathetic voice coming from inside the burqa must have melted even the cussed chowkidar's heart, for he left her alone after that. One by one, all the other passengers left the room until, finally, there were just the two of us left there. She lifted her veil and asked me, 'What time is it?'

'Twelve-thirty,' I replied, and then my voice dried up as I stared at her face. I knew her, but where had I last seen her? Rampur? I stared at her paan-stained teeth and something about the way her mouth curled over the raised canines started tickling my memory.

'Allah tauba!' She laughed and her sunken cheeks dimpled deeply. They seemed to be prodding my memory, saying: 'Come on! Remember this face!'

'I hope I haven't missed the train to Bhagalpur. If I go now, perhaps I can still catch the 25 Dawn . . .' she muttered to herself as she picked up her pathetic baggage and flew out of the door.

'Naseem! Naseem!' I wanted to call out to her, but my

throat was so tight that no sound came out. Her youth had faded exactly like the dhurrie that now held her bedding. Stained and dirty, it was impossible to remember that she was once a laughing beauty. It was obvious that the shop she had opened thirty-two years ago had folded up. No doubt the handsome hockey-stick swinger's photograph had also faded by now in the blue envelope, its scent long evaporated. Would any grandson of a nawab take her home dressed in bridal red? Those young dreams had vanished, and all that was left now was Naseem's ruined beauty, swaddled in the suffocating black of a dirty burqa.

Now that the floodgates of my memory had opened, it all came back to me in a rush. The red salwar, the gossamer dupatta, the saucy gold ring dangling from a delicate nose. Naseem, under the glittering lights of a chandelier, legs tucked under her, palm cupping her ear and singing:

Nathuniya ne, hai Rama, bara dukh deena!
Jab main ho gayi pandrah baras ki,
Godi main mohe dhar leena . . .

A Bengali poet once wrote:

Manush manusher shikari –
Nari korechhe baisya
Purusher korechhe bhikari

Man is the hunter of man –
He is the one who turns a woman into a prostitute
And a man into a beggar

Madhu Ben

If I ever hear a tale of rebirth, believe me, I never laugh. I am convinced such things happen, for I am reminded of an incident that took place years ago in Almora.

It was a bitterly cold winter's evening and it had been snowing steadily all day. The tall pine trees around our house were completely swaddled in a thick white blanket and a hushed silence had descended on the town. We were all huddled round a brazier of hot coals when, suddenly, we heard a knock on the door. Who on earth would venture out on a day like this? We all looked at one another, no one willing to get up and open the door.

'Who is it?' my sister called.

'Open the door,' a woman's voice answered and we looked at one another in amazement. A woman was standing outside in this weather?

I went and opened the door cautiously and then forgot to shut it at what I saw, for before us was a tall and beautiful woman dressed in a Vaishnavi's signature saffron robes. A similar thought immediately crossed our minds: was she that one? Those days, so a rumour went in Almora, an *aghori* tantric Bhairavi had come to town and that she arrived unannounced and took up residence in a house. Her arrival was invariably followed by a spate of tragedies and she left only after the house had been ruined. We had heard about her evil spells, but no one had told us what she looked like. The woman who stood at the door was beautiful and we gazed entranced at her as if she had cast a spell. She carried a small white tin trunk in one hand and wore a saffron silk sari and a matching khand blouse. A thick rope of rudraksha beads hung from her slender neck and her face was framed with short black hair.

'This is the house of Ashwini Kumar Pande, isn't it?' she asked.

'Ye-es,' my elder sister answered in a subdued voice. 'But he is not here, he's gone out.'

'Ba is here, though, isn't she?' she went on.

'Yes,' my sister answered in a puzzled voice. 'Our mother is in the kitchen . . .'

'Fine.' The woman smiled and walked in confidently, past my bemused presence. She put her tin trunk down, took a saffron handkerchief from her pocket and began to wipe the fine dusting of snowflakes from her hair and face. Then, as if she did this every day, she came and made herself comfortable on a small stool and joined us around the fire.

'It is freezing cold here,' she said conversationally. 'If I had known, I'd have brought warmer clothes. I'm frozen in these.' She laughed easily. We gaped at her like idiots, so stunned at the sight of her that none of us thought to move the brazier closer to where she sat or to get her a shawl.

My mother entered the room at this point and, as soon as she saw her, our guest leapt to her feet and bent low over her feet. Ma looked at us in surprise and her eyes asked over the form bent at her feet: 'Who is this?' We waved our hands over our heads to say: 'God knows!'

'Please be seated,' my mother said politely and turned to her servant Jiwaram. 'Jiwa, quickly go and fetch some hot tea from the kitchen,' she ordered.

'Oh, so this is Jiwaram,' our guest said as if she knew all about him. 'The kori whose feet you washed when you married your maid Panchibai to him. You are a great lady, Ba,' she continued. 'You are a high-caste Brahmin, and yet you washed the feet of a lowly kori because you played mother to Panchibai.'

We looked at her in amazement: who was this lady who seemed to know everything about us even though we had never clapped eyes on her before today?

Anyway, after she had been served hot tea, she slid closer to the brazier and said: 'I have come to you with great hope, Ba.' It seemed odd to hear her address our mother as 'Ba', the Gujarati for mother.

'I have come all the way from Rajkot. I am a Gujarati, you see,' she explained.

'Forgive me,' my mother said politely, 'but I don't recall ever having met you there.'

'How could you?' The lady laughed. 'I gave up my

motherland on my own and decided to do my penance by coming here. That is why I seek your help, Ba. I have a distant aunt in Rajkot called Raniyet Ben, who often spoke of you. I believe you two were good friends. At any rate, she is the one who gave me your address. I am in search of a particular family in this town, Ba, and need your help in finding them. Only then will I have performed my act of penance.' She looked earnestly into my mother's face.

'Penance? For what?' My mother seemed as puzzled by her as we were. 'What have you done? Did you accidentally kill a cow? Is that it: is your crime, a *go hatya*?'

'No, not a *go hatya*, Ba, I have committed a worse crime – a *pati hatya*. I killed my own husband.' She sighed deeply. 'And that too, not by accident but knowingly,' she added.

My mother stared at her, disbelief writ all over her face. And in that one instant, the mysterious lady's beauty seemed to peel off in front of our horrified eyes.

'Are you wondering how I can be a Vaishnavi then, despite these saffron clothes and these rudraksha beads? How can I be a murderess – isn't that what you are thinking?' she said. 'I have chosen to punish my body, Ba. There was a time when I rejoiced in draping it with expensive clothes and jewels – you could hardly see my neck for the ropes of diamonds and pearls that hung from it. So, this is where I will start my penance, I decided, and these will be the only ornaments I will henceforth wear . . .' She smiled at us as she fingered the rudraksha beads around her neck.

My mother was still silent.

'Are you wondering why I was never punished if I committed a murder?' the Vaishnavi asked. 'Ba, all I can say is that justice is blind, and because there was no eyewitness to my crime, I escaped any legal action. My husband was a heart patient and diabetes had eaten away at his body the way a colony of termites hollows out a wooden frame. Then a stroke left him incapable of moving and took away his speech . . .'

'But you don't look old enough to have such an aged husband . . .' my mother started to say and then stopped.

'How can I, Ba? I was his fourth wife and a full twenty years younger than him. I was exhausted by the unending nursing that his illness demanded and so, one day, I decided to release him from his miserable life. Do you know what I did?'

We nearly stopped breathing as we waited for the next revelation from our guest. By now the room was pitch dark, even though night had not set in. The storm outside lent a sinister setting to her story. The hair on the nape of my neck stood up as I reflected on the fact that here was a woman who was confessing to a murder before us.

'My husband was losing all his senses, one by one,' she said. 'Yet his hearing, smell and sight had not gone completely. I often used to sing a bhajan for him:

Junu to thayun, re deval, juno to thayun
Mharo hanslo nano ne deval junu
Aa re kaya re hansa, dolvane lagi re
Pari gayan daant maanyili rekhu to rahyun

Tare ne mare hansa, preetyun bandhni re
Uri gayo hanslo pinjar pari re rahyun

This temple, my body, is decrepit now
Yet the swan, my soul, is still young.
The soul is fresh, but the body old.
My teeth are gone, mere stumps remain now.
Ties of love once bound the body and soul together.
But the swan has flown away, leaving just an empty cage.

'And his eyes would start streaming with tears. It was as if he was begging me not to sing that song. I would deliberately switch off the light and tell him frightening ghost stories and sing that song over and over again to frighten him. Sometimes, he would start gagging with fear. Then, one day, I said to him, "Today is amavasya, a moonless night, today is the last day of your life, for I am sure that Yama, the god of death, will send his *doot*, his messengers, to drag you to him tonight."

'He began to tremble and his helpless gaze was fixed on my face. Ever since he had lost his voice and speech, his eyes would speak for him: now they begged me for mercy. That night, when I shone the flashlight in his eyes, I saw his terrified gaze was fixed on the door, as if he expected those messengers to fetch him any moment. I got up silently, pulled a black blanket over myself and stood at the door. Then, in a deep and gruff voice, I said, "Get ready old man, I am Death. I have come to fetch you, you sinner! You robbed your orphaned nephew and caused your widowed sister-in-law to commit suicide. Do you even remember how many poor people you cheated when you took away the goods they had pawned to you? Then you married this innocent young girl by blackmailing her father who owed you money. When he could not pay up, you took his daughter away. The time to pay for your sins has come and I have come to fetch you . . . " And I started to sing that bhajan again, the one that used to reduce him to blubbering jelly, especially the lines at the end: "*Uri gayo hansalo pinjar pari re rahyun*".

'When I woke up the next morning, I saw his lifeless body lying half out of the bed. Perhaps he had tried to run away from that messenger of death. The swan had truly flown away, Ba.' She looked at my mother. 'After that, he came and stood at my bedside each night. He didn't speak a word or call out my name. He just stared at me with terrified eyes and I went cold with fear. His death had made me the mistress of millions, but I seemed to have lost my sleep, my peace of mind – indeed, my appetite and thirst as well. Someone told me to do a shraddha at Pretshila, saying that this would give peace to his wandering spirit, but nothing helped. However, after I did the shraddha, he spoke to me. "You wicked woman," he said. "You killed me. The shraddha you performed for the peace of my soul at Gaya is only half done. Go straight to Almora, to the family where I have been reborn. Confess your crime to all you meet there, rub your head against my feet in front of everyone there. And then, when you look into my eyes, you will know whether I have finally forgiven you."

'You will take me there, won't you, Ba?' she pleaded. 'This is the family's name . . .' She named it. 'That is the house my husband has taken rebirth in.' She produced a crumpled piece of paper with an address scribbled on it, waving it in front of my mother's face.

Almora was such a small town in those days that it was not difficult at all to locate the address our guest had produced. My mother had sent word to them that someone called Madhu Ben had come from Gujarat to meet the family where she believed her late husband had taken rebirth. Naturally, she drew a discreet veil over other parts of the story.

The next day, we all got dressed to visit the family. A small crowd of interested onlookers had already gathered and filled the courtyard. Madhu Ben's face assumed an anxious, sombre expression and her eyes restlessly combed the faces in front of her. Our host understood who she sought and said, 'Come, the child has just shut his eyes. He is in the inner room.'

Madhu Ben was like a woman possessed: she broke away from our group and almost ran along with the man. We followed her into the house, the curious onlookers behind us. The baby was lying in a large basket. His innocent face in sleep was rosy and pink and his small hands were bunched up in fists, close to his ears. Madhu Ben fell at his feet and burst into loud wails: 'Tell me, tell me, have you forgiven me? I killed you, I . . .' She clung to the baby's feet so hard that I was afraid she would crush them.

Our host looked at us sternly, as if to ask why we had

not told him that this woman was a murderess, how we dared to bring such a woman to a decent man's house. His angry gaze accused my mother of concealing the truth from him. Startled by the uproar, the baby's mother came from the next room and clutched the baby to her breast. Madhu Ben fell at the mother's feet. 'Please spare a moment for my story, then you can take the baby away. Please,' she babbled. And then she repeated to the entire crowd the same story she had told us the previous evening.

Something about Madhu Ben's personality and her amazing story, coupled with the fact that she freely confessed her crime, held the attention of everyone present there. And, miraculously, she managed to turn the hostility that had emanated from our host into a wave of sympathy. Even the mother of the baby sat down, enraptured by the strange tale of Madhu Ben's crime.

Madhu Ben frantically kissed the baby's feet. 'Look at me, please,' she pleaded. 'Tell me you have forgiven me . . .'

And then, to our consternation, the baby opened its eyes and turned its clear gaze on Madhu Ben's face. It did not weep or whimper or get restive; suddenly, it gave her a lovely toothless smile. In the hills, we believe that when babies smile or cry in their sleep, they remember their past life. It certainly seemed as if we were witnessing something like that now. God knows whether it remembered its past life or whether this was indeed the omen that Madhu Ben had been seeking.

She jumped with joy. 'I knew it,' she exclaimed exultantly. 'I knew that you would forgive me,' she told the baby.

Then, without another glance at any of us, or even a word of thanks to my mother, she kissed the baby's feet once more and ran out of the house.

She had reached home before us and was standing, ready to leave, her trunk in her hand. 'How do I even thank you, Ba?' she asked my mother. 'You have helped lift a huge burden off my chest. Did you see how he smiled and forgave me? May I leave now?'

'But how can you leave now, Madhu Ben?' my mother said. 'There is no bus to Kathgodam at this hour. You will only be able to leave tomorrow morning . . .'

Madhu Ben's face fell at this piece of information. 'Ba, I must leave today. I have secured his forgiveness and it seems wrong to be under the same sky, in the same town, and sleep in separate beds.'

My god, I thought, now this mad woman will ask us to take her there again. But she didn't do that. She sat on our terrace for a long time that night and gazed at the snow-covered peaks in the horizon. I went and sat next to her and she put her arm lovingly around my neck. 'Sleep with me tonight. I'll tell you wonderful stories.'

I ran. Suppose this creature told me another of her macabre ghost stories and killed me? I had no desire to add another number to her sins.

Madhu Ben's bus was to leave at eight in the morning. Ma was getting her breakfast ready and I was helping her roll the puris when Madhu Ben entered the kitchen, singing in a high, sweet voice.

'*Juno to thayun, deval*' – she entered warbling – '*juno to thaiyun* . . .'

Mrs Ghose

This morning, my eyes alighted on a news item: 'Maidservant robs her employer of fifteen thousand and flees'. My eyes didn't linger, for, after all, every day one reads of robberies, thefts and burglaries. We react only if the amount runs in lakhs or where the script is straight out of a film, with the *dhishoom-dhishoom* kind of fights thrown in. Where, for instance, the robbers lob tear gas shells or attack bank guards with knives and guns or where professional thugs relieve train passengers of all their worldly goods. No one, it seems, even tries to chase these fellows, and trains run on schedule as if this is an everyday occurrence.

Then, suddenly, my eyes fell on the name of the maid. My god, was this the same Mrs Ghose I had once met? Wasn't this the name she called herself? If she was the same woman, then for a minute I sent a silent prayer of thanks to her for not honouring me with a second visit. Had she come again, and had I sent her off to my daughter, we might have had our names in the papers today!

Last summer, I was lying in my room one afternoon when the doorbell rang. I opened the door and before me stood a woman wearing a clean white sari with no border, and a white blouse. She had a plastic bag in one hand and I thought for a moment that she was one of those door-to-door salesgirls who sell shampoo, washing soap or incense sticks. Before I could say anything, she smiled at me and asked me in Bengali: 'May I come in?' There was something about her clean looks and her smile – I found it difficult to deny her entry.

'Do you have any work with me?' I asked her.

'I've heard that you speak beautiful Bengali, that is why I've come all this way to meet you.' She smiled.

'Who told you I speak Bengali?' I asked her.

'My uncle heard your lecture on Saratchandra at the Bengali Club and said he hadn't heard such chaste Bengali for a long time,' she replied. Naturally, I was flattered and looked closely at her. She must have been middle-aged, but her face was smooth and clear, with no trace of any lines or wrinkles. Her austere white clothes gave her the bearing of a genteel woman, but there was something about her eyes that was not quite right. I felt as if her clothes and expression were a deliberately cultivated costume. Anyhow, I let her in.

'I am a very unhappy woman,' she began without preamble and burst into tears almost as soon as she sat down. I was completely nonplussed. 'I beg of you, please help me find a job,' she pleaded. 'I am ready to wash, cook, do anything, if I can work in a decent home where they treat me with respect. I don't even want a salary – just food and clean clothes are enough,' she concluded.

For a moment I was taken aback – where does one find such people any more? Almost before you can open your mouth to offer a salary, a prospective maid nowadays wants to know how many people she will have to cook for, what her wages will be, how many free days she can expect and so on.

'Where do you stay?' I asked.

'In Latouche Road,' she replied. 'With a distant uncle. My father worked for the Railways and married me to a loco worker. My husband used to get epileptic fits and was crushed under a train. Ever since, I have nobody.'

'Are you willing to work in another town?' I asked her, moved by her story. 'My daughter lives in Chandigarh, I could send you to her.'

'O ma!' she exclaimed in Bengali. 'Why would I not go? Of course I'm ready,' she said and wrung my hands in gratitude. 'I'll come here tomorrow with my things and my uncle. I want you to meet him, he was so impressed with you that day!' Then she hesitated and said, 'But I have to ask you for a favour . . .' and stopped, smiling shyly at me.

'What is it?' I prodded her.

'If you can lend me some money, I'll buy myself some washing soap. How can I go there with dirty clothes on me? There is also the rickshaw fare from Latouche Road to your place,' she stammered.

I opened my purse and handed her what she asked for, not even once reflecting that never before in my life had I set eyes on this woman. She opened her carry bag to put the money in, then hesitated once more. '*Dayamayi* (kind one),' she said softly. 'There is another request – just look at this.' She lifted her sari to show me her petticoat, patched and darned in a number of places. 'If you can give me some more money, I'll get two petticoats stitched by tomorrow. I feel ashamed that I have been reduced to begging even for such things,' she said and her eyes filled up with tears.

I handed her another note.

I have never seen her since. Perhaps it has taken the poor woman all this time to do her laundry – she must have accumulated a load of dirty linen. I kept my foolishness to myself; what could I have said in defence of my generosity? Suddenly, when I read that name, a bell rang and I remembered an incident I had all but forgotten. I can barely recall her face now, but I do remember she had a mole on her left cheek, a scar on her forehead and large eyes, ever ready to weep. Those I remember as clearly as the two crisp notes I handed over to her.

Pagaliya

There is a road that leads to the cantonment in Lucknow, with a narrow bridge straddling a railway line beneath. Known as the Katai ka Pul – the Bridge of Beheadings – it has a strange story behind its name. They say a British Army officer's pretty wife was once having a raging affair with her handsome young coachman. One day, the husband caught them red-handed, pulled out his revolver and started to shoot at them in anger. The coachman managed to dodge the bullets and fled, but the pretty wife died on the spot. The cuckolded husband was so overcome with remorse at having killed his wife that he put the revolver to his temple and shot himself as well, blowing his head clean off his body. Ever since, so the story goes, his headless ghost roams the area after midnight and has often been spotted by passers-by. Some, in fact, have reported that the sahib asks terrified wayfarers for a bottle of beer and fried fish. The spot, perhaps because it is so narrow, has also seen several accidents, and the superstitious promptly ascribe all these to the curse of the headless sahib.

I myself have seen at least seven or eight bodies splayed on the tracks below. One of them was a dear neighbour, Mr Sen. One night, close to midnight, he suddenly left his house without telling anyone. The next morning, he was found dead under the bridge. His wife says he thought someone was calling him. To date, no one has been able to give a satisfactory explanation for his mysterious death. The superstitious, of course, say that the headless sahib beckons victims to their death. At any rate, the spot is notorious all over Lucknow for its gory history and is considered one of the most dangerous crossroads of the city. One road leads to the Dilkusha Gardens and, all night, reckless lorry drivers drive on it like the wind. The other road leads to the houses of the cantonment, the third heads to the airport and the fourth to Sadar Bazaar. Needless to say, there is heavy traffic on all four roads and, since this is also the way to the Dilkusha Gardens, a favourite morning walkers' spot. I have been crossing the bridge for years on my morning walk and sometimes even late at night to go to a chemist's shop nearby. But never have I seen the headless sahib. However, I have seen a few headless bodies there and it is about one of them that I write.

When I first saw her, her hair was not cropped the way it is now. About twenty-four or five years old, she was like any high-spirited young woman. She had a round face, large, limpid eyes and a sharp nose. A wicked smile always danced on her lips. When they saw her, women invariably averted their gaze, but as soon as a man passed by, the young woman would try and attract his attention. I asked my maid about her: who was this person who sat on the Katai ka Pul nowadays? I had never seen her in the area before.

'She's a real baggage.' My maid sniffed disapprovingly. 'When you were away, we had managed to drive her out of the colony, but she's come back again, the harlot!'

'Why?' I asked her. 'Why had you all driven her out? She doesn't harm anyone, just sits there all day, muttering and smiling to herself. Poor thing, looks like a mad woman abandoned by her family. Give her two rotis from today.'

'Never,' she said vehemently. 'She is bad news, that one. All the young boys and men gather around her and she cackles with glee at her power, the bitch. God knows where she's arrived from! Be a good thing if the headless sahib were to come and take her away one day,' she added spitefully.

So she continued to sit there, fed by some kind passers-by. Someone had placed a broken china mug near her and the neighbouring dhaba owner would send her some tea from time to time. Someone had also given her an old shawl to cover herself with, but the mad woman reacted sharply to anyone trying to cover her body. She'd flung the shawl away at first, then pick it up to tie it turban-like on her head. I was most curious to find out who she was and where she had come from, what had turned her mind crazy, but never found the courage to speak to her. I also knew she hated all women.

Then, one day, I was returning from a nearby temple

that I often visited. I gave her some prasad and she threw it back into my face, crudely screaming: 'Scram!' and made an insulting gesture. I had barely recovered from this when a phalanx of army recruits went jogging by. The mad woman clapped her hands delightedly, openly flaunting her body at them, her hands making lewd gestures. I was so repelled by her blatant soliciting that I left in disgust. My maid was right, after all, I thought. This one deserved to be driven away from our neighbourhood.

Finally, she solved the problem herself. Our neighbourhood ration shop employed a cadaverous young man for doling out rice and sugar. He was called Rambadan (literally, the embodiment of the Lord's body), but a more misplaced name was never seen. His face was like that of an ogre and it topped a body that had rickety arms and legs. Above all, his gaze, sly and darting, was like that of a crafty crow. Then one day, my maid informed me that Rambadan had taken the mad woman of the puliya to his home. He had married her at the nearby temple, she sniffed. His home? I asked her. Does he even have a roof to call his own? He used to sleep outside the ration shop under a tin roof at night and double as its watchman. Pagaliya, as the mad woman was called by the servants, joined him there. Slowly, I saw, Rambadan bought her new clothes, some bright chunris, bindis for her forehead, surma for her eyes and missi for her teeth. A little brazier was his next gift, and then followed some vessels for cooking. The ration shop was right outside my terrace and I could not help peering into the new life that was sprouting under the tin roof outside it. Occasionally, the aroma of basmati rice floated to my nostrils from their little kitchen, and once in a while, the heavenly scent of a good meat curry. I had known Rambadan for years, so I called out to him one day. 'So, Rambadan,' I teased him. 'Is there a wedding feast being cooked at home today?' The poor man blushed and turned his face away. He had become the butt of the entire colony's teasing of late.

'What feast, Bahuji?' he answered, 'we are poor people. Today, that one' – he refused to take her name – 'insisted that she wanted to eat rice and meat curry, so . . .' He left the sentence unfinished. 'That one' glowered at me from where she sat presiding over the bubbling pot, as if to say: 'Who are you to ask us what we are eating and why? What we cook and eat is our business.'

It was not long before Rambadan's pinched face acquired a healthy glow. Pagaliya filled out too and became prettier by the day. Each time she covered her head with her red chunariya and jangled her bangles to go somewhere, her jealous husband would follow her. I had to leave for London soon after Rambadan married his love, and heard on my return that one day Pagaliya went out to relieve herself and never returned. Rambadan waited up for her all night, but there was no sign of her. When I went for my first morning walk after my return, I saw poor Rambadan stretched out on his cot, his blank gaze fixed on the roof of his ruined Taj Mahal. His hands were locked under his head and he lay there like a corpse. I avoided him, feeling wretched for his condition.

The next day, when I went past his hovel, I noticed he wasn't there. The third day, I saw a huge crowd outside his 'home'. Maddened with grief, I learnt, my poor Shah Jahan had killed himself by jumping off the Katai ka Pul. We all collected money for his last rites and some kind souls went and cremated him. Soon, he became a memory and another helping hand replaced Rambadan at the ration shop.

Then, suddenly, Pagaliya arrived one day, like a meteor out of the blue. She went and sat down under the little tin roof and no one had the heart to dislodge her. I see her there every day. She still turns her face away at the sight of women, but if a man passes by, her eyes light up. Almost every day, I see the same drama enacted: a man passes Pagaliya and she makes an inviting gesture. His bicycle wobbles for a moment. Some pass on, others look around furtively to see if anyone is looking. Then, he gets off his bicycle and starts to chat her up. Knowing full well that this is a woman who is alone and deranged, these men wait to get their oar in.

One day, if one of them rapes her, no court of law will accept her version of the episode, for she is mad, after all. One day, some man will take advantage of Pagaliya, I know, that is the poor woman's destiny.

Lalita

One of Rabindranath Tagore's works describes a woman called Lalita, who blew through life like the spring breeze. Just such a woman – interestingly, she was called Lalita too – blew once through our lives as well.

It was a blisteringly hot summer afternoon in Orchha, and we were restlessly tossing on straw mats spread on the cool floor of a darkened room, when our old maid Jagrani brought her daughter Lalita into the room. 'Here she is, Binnoo,' she said. 'This bundle of trouble has run away once again from her husband's house.' Lalita came and fell at our feet, 'Ai, Jijji!' She sobbed. 'Keep me here, near these feet, I swear I'll never go back!' My head reeled with the odour from her dirty clothes. Her hair was matted and god knows when she had last washed the smelly mustard oil from it. She lay there, sobbing, as Jagrani provided us with a commentary of her daughter's life to date. 'That unfeeling butcher' – she wept, referring to Lalita's husband – 'he nearly thrashed her to death. Just take a look at this!'

She took the rags off Lalita's back. We gasped in horror as we saw the angry weals there: he had branded her with red-hot tongs and then thrown her out. There was no question of sending Lalita back to her torturer; she was back in our lives for good.

More than her mother, Lalita had been our constant companion. She taught us how to hitch our saris up to our knees and climb tamarind trees and to pick smooth pebbles from the Betwa that flowed near our haveli. She would grind fresh henna leaves and then decorate out hands with the paste. No doll could get married without Lalita's expert help: she cooked the feast, dressed the bride and groom and then sang all the wedding songs. Her voice rang high over the courtyard with sweet Bundelkhandi folk songs and gathered an audience in minutes.

Then, one day, we had to bid Lalita goodbye: she was just twelve, but Jagrani was in a hurry to send her to her husband's home. Like most little girls in Bundelkhand, Lalita had been a child bride, and now it was time for her to leave for her husband's home. Since she spent all her time with us, we had made her take off the heavy silver ornaments that weighed her feet and ankles down and made her wear clean clothes. Dark and lissom, Lalita was a pretty little thing until you came close to her. Then you realized that she had lost one eye to smallpox. It was probably this flaw that created trouble between her husband and her: he never forgave his family for marrying him off to a one-eyed bride. Every other month, Lalita would run away to her mother, unable to take more thrashing from her cruel husband, a middle-aged shepherd who had been given a handsome dowry by Jagrani and her husband. Perhaps because she had been thrashed so often since she was small, Lalita cheerfully faced every adversity that life served her.

'Tell us, Lalita' – we would tease her – 'when you look so pretty in your clean clothes, why does that shepherd thrash you?' In answer, she would point a finger to her blind eye and sing:

This wretched eye is my sorrow
It is the cause of my exile . . .

Her lovely voice, with just a hint of a sob and a laugh, soared over the courtyard and people smiled as they heard it. Whatever sadness Lalita carried within her, she never let it colour her zest for life.

Bundelkhand has several peculiar traditions; one of them is the mandatory wailing when a bride leaves her mother's home for her father-in-law's. The same wailing takes place when she arrives at her mother's on a visit as well. It is difficult to recreate in words what this sounds like: it is a falling and rising and singing all rolled into one wail. Loud and clear, this wail would float over the neighbourhood whenever a girl was bid goodbye and sent to her father-in-law's home. The moment the wails reached our ears, we ran to the terrace and leant over the edge to hear the words and giggle at them. '*Ai-ai-ai, maiyya ree*' – it started – 'they have called me-e-e-e . . .'

'Poor thing,' I said once to Lalita, who was watching the spectacle along with us. 'She sounds really mournful.'

'*Hunh!*' Lalita spat in disgust. 'Call this wailing? Just listen to me!' So saying, she took off. Within minutes, she had covered her face with her sari end and her eyes streamed as she improvised hilarious permutations of that wail.

'*Ai-ai-ai, maiyya ree*,' she started. 'If you send me away today, I'll run back tomorrow, *ai-e-e*! I've left some sweets hidden in an alcove in my room, *ai-e-e, maiyya*, don't let my sister-in-law get at them, *ai-e-e* . . .' She went on and on, gathering new ideas as she wailed. We finally got her to stop, conceding gladly that she was a champion in the department of wailing. She stopped and smiled triumphantly. 'That is what is called wailing,' she told us. 'And you thought that was good! *Hunh!*'

Jagrani heard of her daughter's performance. 'It's true, Binnoo,' she said. 'Do you know, Lalita's fame has spread to the villages around and they send their daughters to her to learn the art of true wailing!'

Wailing was also mandatory at deaths; so every time there was a death in the town, Lalita was summoned to lead the chorus of wails. Lalita claimed that her wails were so effective that even the dead man's enemies were moved to tears. Naturally, Lalita was a fabulous singer. What a fund of folk songs that girl had! *Tona*, *Chhand*, *Phag*, *Birha* – all these would tumble out effortlessly from her throat at the right occasions. Often, she composed her own lines, using her imagination to produce beautiful images and conceits. Her curiosity was boundless: she saw us rubbing cold cream on our faces one day and asked: '*Hai*, Jijji, what on earth is that?'

'Cream,' said my sister. 'You rub it into your face to stop it from chapping in winter and it keeps your skin smooth and fair.'

'*Hai*, Jijji,' she begged. 'Give me some too. Do you know, someone once asked Winter: "Where are you off to?" and Winter said: 'To make the fair dark and the dark miserable." Help this dark one, Jijji.' She smiled.

How could one refuse such a charming request? Ever since Lalita had declared that she would never go back to her cruel shepherd and spend the rest of her life with us, we became her world. When we went to Almora in summer, she insisted that she would go with us to see the land of snow. When we got off the train at Kathgodam and she got her first glimpse of the mountains, she almost fainted. '*Baap re baap*,' she said in awe. 'Just look at them! And Jijji' – she turned to us – 'why do the clouds in your land smoke?' As our car went up the turns and twists to Almora, Lalita turned in fury to the driver, '*Ai*, driver sahib, did you have toddy for breakfast? Can't you keep the motor straight?' We shushed her, but each time the car took a sharp turn and she fell sideways onto the driver, she'd mutter curses at him. 'Look at the bastard, he's laughing at me! I'm telling you, Jijji' – she'd turn to face us – 'this wretched fool is going to kill us today!'

She breathed a sigh of relief when we finally reached Almora, but if we had hoped that Lalita would be moved to poetry at the sight of our magnificent mountains, we were in for a surprise. '*Hunh!*' she said dismissively. 'What do your precious mountains do except breathe snow down their sides?' My elder sister Jayanti felt that Lalita was getting out of hand and decided to teach her to read and write. But getting her to write the alphabet was a nightmare. Unhappy with just the two strokes that came out of the Hindi alphabet 'A', Lalita added two more to make it like the four arms of Brahma and then added some leaves and flowers to them. 'What is this, Lalita?' my sister scolded her. 'Can't you just copy what I've written down?'

'Hunh, Jijji,' she replied, gazing lovingly at her artwork. 'I've just decorated the poor thing.' Nothing we did could make her change her attitude to writing and she took two full months to just graduate to the third letter of the alphabet. Finally, she got fed up. 'Enough!' she declared decisively one morning, throwing the primer aside. 'I've had enough of this rubbish! I'd rather learn how to stitch, Jijji!' So we got her an embroidery frame, some skeins of silk, needles and cloth, and someone traced a parrot onto the cloth for her to embroider into a pair of pillow cases. Something in the act of sewing got Lalita pensive and we realized how deeply she missed her old life. She'd sit there with the needlework lying forgotten in her lap and say: 'The black cow must have had her calf by now, don't you think?' Or, 'It is time for the Suata fair in my husband's village, all the girls must be getting ready for it. Next month, there will be one near the Kundeswar Mahadev temple . . .'

Finally, one of us said: 'If you miss that man's village so much, why don't you go back to your precious shepherd, Lalita?' Lalita reared up like a spitting cobra: 'May his bones rot!' she started. 'May his eyes be blinded by pox! Who said I miss that evil one?' And she went back to her work.

It was nearing winter and time for our family to return to Orchha when we noticed how excited Lalita was. She'd run and cheerfully perform every task and started counting the days to our return. On the journey back to Tikamgarh, Lalita cursed each time the train stopped at a station. 'Now what is the matter?' she'd scold the train and get up to push the walls of our compartment. 'Come on, move, you whore! Look at her fussing!' She turned to us for corroboration. 'May your husband die, you whore, you stupid harlot!' And when the train refused to be moved by her hail of curses, Lalita let fly another string of colourful abuses. The whole compartment rocked with laughter at her and Lalita turned her fury on them. 'Go on, laugh, you idiots! If you can wait patiently to reach your own homes, why did you not travel by bullock cart? I wish I had taken one, at least I'd have got the bullock to listen to me! One kick on its backside, and it would have run!'

Her entire family had assembled at the station to receive her and Lalita wailed in ecstasy as she embraced them one by one. One year with us in the hills had filled her out: her cheeks glowed with healthy colour and her body was ripe with youth. When she wore her sari tucked between her legs like other Bundelkhandi women and tied her long hair into a neat bun, people turned their heads to give her another look. She had learnt to cover her bad eye with her sari and flirted effectively with just one. Soon after our return, she went to the Kundeswar Mahadev fair with her family, and her old shepherd, unable to believe that this was his scruffy wife, fell in love with her. He came with folded hands to our house and begged us to give him another chance. 'I swear by the waters of the holy Ganga,' he promised my mother, 'I will keep her like a queen, Annadata. Just give me another chance.'

So she went with him, but not before she had made him grovel before her. For years after we went to Santiniketan, my sister and I remembered her funny antics and wondered where she was and how she was doing. Four years later, we went back to Orchha. The minute Jagrani heard we had come, she came running to meet us. 'How is Lalita?' was our first question. Jagrani covered her eyes with her sari and started to sob. 'That unfortunate child!' She sobbed. 'She had three children in three years, Binnoo, not one survived, and the third one took my Lalita with him as well.'

We were stunned. I remembered how she had once said to me: '*Ai*, Jijji, when I die, put a shroud of *charchet* on my bier, all right?'

'What on earth is *charchet*, you silly thing?' I had asked.

'That material that Ba sahib (the rani of Orchha) has made her car curtains out of,' she explained.

Lalita had wanted a shroud of red georgette. Poor thing! 'They wrapped her poor body in cheap cotton, Jijji,' Jagrani wailed. 'That butcher did not even buy her a decent shroud!'

All of us were silent, each remembering Lalita's happy

smiling, face and her funny antics. Lalita with one hand on her ear, singing:

> This wretched eye is my sorrow
> It is the cause of my exile . . .

Her end was not unlike Tagore's heroine's. 'Disrespect destroyed you, poor Lalita,' says Tagore. It was what destroyed our Lalita as well.

A Mother's Prayer

So long as a man's self-confidence is inviolate, his pride remains intact. He feels no need to bow his head before anyone else. It is only when he feels that all doors around him are closing that he turns in despair to God. In our shastras, this refuge is what is called *Sharanagati* or *Prapatti* and indicates that the solace such a haven offers is not unlike the security that an infant finds at a mother's breast.

Kumaon has one such haven for those who have despaired of life or human justice. The walls of this temple are festooned with thousands of letters that are desperate appeals addressed to God. When this appeal is heard and justice received, the grateful supplicant returns, ritually tears up his letter and offers a bell to Gwala Devta, the dispenser of this divine justice. Chitai, where this quaint temple is situated, is a mere four miles from Almora. Perched on top of a hill, the tinkle of the temple's bells swaying in the breeze can be heard from the path that leads up to it. Red and white flags flutter in the brisk breeze that always blows around here and the sounds of the myriad bells vary from the deep boom to a gentle tinkle. Each bell has the name of the grateful donor inscribed on it. 'This bell was offered by Parvati Rautela of Sunai village to Gwala Devta. He saved her husband Ganga Singh Rautela from the gallows,' reads one. 'This bell was offered by the brothers Kheem Singh and Aan Singh,' says another. Who were these brothers and what did the Gwala Devta do for them? Although there was no embellishment of this cryptic inscription, I always imagined that they too were saved from the noose. Virtually every other bell is offered by those who had no hope of escaping death by hanging. All over Kumaon, the devout believe that Gwala Devta's justice is always weighed in favour of the pure of heart. They say he has the uncanny ability to separate water from milk. However, if the supplicant is truly guilty, Gwala Devta's punishment is equally swift.

There is a marvellous sense of peace within the little temple. A small image of Bhairav is studded on one wall and is barely visible behind the thick swirls of smoke from incense and the lamps of ghee that burn constantly. Dark, almost womb-like, the temple of Gwala Devta preserves a certain air of mysteriousness that cannot but evoke awe. Whenever I go to Almora, I make it a point to visit this temple and on each trip I make it a point to read some of the letters hung in bunches all around the main temple. Who are these fearless people who pronounce their crime so freely to the world and what gives them this courage? Is it the fear of imminent death that makes them shed their modesty and diffidence?

This time when I visited the temple, three letters caught my attention. One was written in Bengali: '*Thakur, bipade morey rokkha koro. Ami khoon korini . . .*' (Thakur, protect me in my time of danger. I have not committed the murder). Under this appeal, in neat letters, was the name of the supplicant: Neelkanth Goswami. The second letter was attached to the court order pronouncing a death sentence. The letter, written in the charming and slightly ornate old-fashioned Pahari style, began thus: '*Swasti Sri Sarvopama Yogya Sri Gwala Devta . . .*' – as if the writer, one Dungar Singh, were addressing an elder in his family. What followed was a graphic account of his crime. He had killed his beautiful young wife and, as I read the letter, I felt as if I could almost see the blood dripping from the head he had hacked off her neck. 'Tell me, Gwala Devta,' Dungar Singh wrote. 'If you had been in my place, would you not have hacked off the neck of this wicked *khasini*, like the goat we kill at your doorstep? I nursed her back to health after three years of tuberculosis and she paid me back by conspiring to kill me. That too, with my own brother's help! I caught her red-handed and did what any red-blooded thakur male could do, Gwala Devta,' Dungar Singh wrote. 'Now you give your verdict on who was wrong and who was not.'

The third letter was the most amazing of all. It was written in a childish schoolgirl's hand and on a page torn from a school notebook. I stiffened as I read the opening line: 'Gwaladev, if there is any truth in your power, make my daughter a widow!'

What mother was this, I thought, to ask for such a boon? Plead for her own daughter to be made a widow?

But as I read her impassioned appeal, I felt this was a boon that Gwala Devta would be forced to grant. Her only daughter, the mother wrote, was like a tender flower, but the monster who had married did not give her a day's happiness. Along with his mother, he had tortured her, burning her with live coals. When she had asked to go and visit her mother's home, he had burnt her tongue so that her mouth was a mess of sores. Finally, he broke her legs. Her parents brought their half-dead daughter home and, maddened with grief, the mother had come with her appeal to the only true dispenser of justice she could think of: Gwala Devta. 'I brought her home yesterday,' she said. 'I want justice, Gwaladev. Let the bastard suffer the same fate as my daughter. Don't grant him an easy death, Gollu, let him inch towards his end in misery. The day my daughter becomes a widow, Gollu,' she promised, 'I'll come and sacrifice a goat at your doorstep. Rather than have a husband like hers, I wish her widowhood, my Lord!'

That childish scrawl contained the sorrow of countless mothers in Kumaon. That such women should have to seek justice at the court of Gwala Devta rather than at a court of law, I thought to myself, was enough cause for all of us to lower our heads in shame.

Binnu

When I first saw her, I must confess I was a trifle disappointed. How could this be her? She had a plain face, a thin body and her clothes were quite ordinary. Then, suddenly, she smiled and it was as if a dead tree had suddenly burst into flower. Her smile danced from her lips to her eyes and dimples and drenched her whole personality with its radiance.

'I've brought you *chapetas*. You had asked for them, right?' she said and spread her palm to reveal a set of brightly coloured dice, patterned in bright red lacquer. Her outspread palm invited me to join her in a game straightaway. That is how we first met each other.

Like most young girls of my age in those times, I loved playing gitti with a set of lacquered chapetas and stealing raw mangoes from the orchards around our home in Orchha. Binnu and I discovered that we could do both together very well. When the burning summer sun had everyone take refuge behind closed doors, she would quietly creep into my room by the back door and whisper: 'Ai, Chhoti Jijji, want to play a game of chapeta with me? See what I have brought for you today.' And then she would undo a corner of her sari to show me the raw green mangoes stolen that morning.

'Come' – she tempted me with these promised delights – 'let's quickly play a hand while your mother is asleep. Come!'

She was terrified of my mother and, for some reason, my mother hated my playing with her. 'How many times have I warned you to not let that girl into the house?' she had shouted when she first caught us together. 'Don't ever let me see her here again. She is a snake, I know, a viper's spawn. God knows how many homes mother and daughter have ruined. And you play that horrible game with her! Haven't I warned you that slapping the earth invites bad luck? They say you get caught in an eternal cycle of debt if you do, and that is what your gitti-playing is all about. Toss those lacquer dice on your fingers and see how thick and misshapen they will become later.' She wagged her own slim finger at me. 'Who will I find to marry you then?'

Yet, whenever Binnu crept into my life, I promptly forgot my mother's warnings and we'd start playing gitti like two addicts. Binnu used to creep in wearing a stiffly starched chador and I can still recall the perfume she exuded. Hina, khus, kewra, musk – it seemed as if she poured all these into the starch when she dipped that chador in it. The perfume lingered in my room even after she left and my mother's sharp nose picked it up immediately.

'Who'd come here this afternoon?' she asked one day.

'That same *dhingri*, isn't it? Very well then, from tomorrow you are to sleep in my room in the afternoons.' So, for the next two or three months, my companion and I were unable to meet. Then, just before the summer holidays ended, we went to the local fair at the Kundeswar Mahadev temple. I could smell Binnu before I spotted her and ran towards her. She had just finished buying some bright green bangles and I could hear them tinkling on her thin wrists. She moved on to a neighbouring tattoo-maker's stall and started haggling over the prices of a tattoo. 'I want Radha-Krishna on one arm and three beauty spots on my chin. And I won't pay you a penny more than two rupees,' she was telling him.

'I'll pay you two rupees and more if I can hold your chin in my hands, Sarkar,' the bold artist replied. I was stunned at this shameless flirting and wondered whether my mother was right after all. This friend, who could win hands down in a game of gitti and sing the most haunting *Phag* songs, the girl who could climb trees and throw down raw mangoes to me below – was she really someone else when I was not there? If she wasn't, why didn't she slap down the man's shameless proposition and walk off? I saw her take out the money to pay off the bangle seller and then tilt her chin towards the tattoo man, who caressed its soft roundness before he started to prick it.

Suddenly, I lost my appetite for the razzle-dazzle of the stalls, so I quietly slipped away to the banks of the nearby stream that ran by the temple. I dipped my feet into the water and was cooling them when she arrived like a hurricane and hugged me. 'Look at her! Here I was, looking everywhere in the fairground, and where do I find her? Near the stream!' She laughed. The familiar perfume from her chador tickled my nostrils. 'Look, Chhoti Jijji, I got this tattoo done today! Like it?' And she tilted her chin for me to admire.

The skin was slightly sore where three neat beauty spots had been inked in. Her eyes were darkened with surma and lips stained with the paan she was chewing. I have to say, she looked very pretty.

'Why are you sulking, Jijji?' she asked when I refused to answer.

When I still did not unbend, she went on: 'What can I do? Maaji (that is what she called my mother) has forbidden me to come to your kothi, and perhaps she is right, Jijji. No good home welcomes the likes of us; we are shooed away like pariah dogs from homes such as yours.' She turned her face away to hide her tears.

I melted. 'Binnu,' I replied, holding her wrist, 'is it true what they say about you?' I knew she would not lie to me.

'What do they say, Jijji?' she asked me innocently, placing her wrist on my lap. I stared down at it to see the freshly tattooed lovers Radha-Krishna flutter in my lap. '*Jai Radhe-Shyam*' was tattooed underneath in praise of the divine lovers. God knows what that man had extracted from her for this work of art!

'Don't pretend you don't know!' I burst out. 'Look at me!' I tried to pull her face towards me, but she burrowed her head into my lap, weeping.

I don't know how long I sat there, holding her head in my lap, for it was almost dark when we got up. She had said nothing to me, but her silence had revealed everything. There was little point in seeking further answers now.

I learnt of her strange life story much later. She was married off when she was just eight and then packed off to her husband's home when she turned ten. Suddenly, she found that she was now considered a responsible young woman. Confused by chores she was unable to perform and the demands of a randy husband, she discovered that her childhood had come to an abrupt end. One day, after her mother-in-law had thrashed her soundly, she slipped away from her husband's bed and ran away. She was young and pretty and, what is more, she also knew the hunger she could arouse in men and how to feed it.

Binnu sang like a bird, so soon word spread about this pretty young girl who had a huge repertoire of folk songs and she began to be invited to sing at births and thread ceremonies and on festivals like Holi and the temple's feast days. She'd arrive, settle herself behind the dholak and so captivate her listeners that people began to whisper about her. Someone said that she had become the mistress of some rich feudal lord in the area, someone else added that another lover's unhappy wife, unable to bear the indignity of rejection, had taken poison and killed herself. Once, Binnu was spirited away by a Parsi contractor to Bombay for a pleasure trip and someone spotted her there, wearing high heels and lipstick! Shameless hussy, they hissed. But all this only succeeded in making Binnu into a sort of trophy that people vied to display at weddings and other ceremonies. If she got up to dance, people forgot to go and eat their dinner. They swore she was an enchantress who could mesmerize her audience into not moving for hours.

Riding high on her fame, Binnu added the bawdy songs of Bundelkhand's legendary folk singer Isuri to her repertoire. Soon, young girls and women stopped coming for her performances, stuffing their fingers in their ears to protect themselves from such vulgar words. 'Keep quiet, you shameless hussy!' she was told, but their curses only made Binnu naughtier. She deliberately sang even randier songs to drive those moral policewomen away, laughing openly at their discomfort. Like Corbett's furious man-eating tigress who, having tasted human blood, could no longer be satisfied with tame game, there was no stopping Binnu now.

After that riverside meeting with her, I left for Santiniketan and was away for many years. I met Binnu next at my own wedding when my mother invited her to sing one evening. By now, Binnu was a professional singer with her own band of accompanists. She saw me dressed as a bride-to-be and hugged me as warmly as ever. 'So, Chhoti Jijji, it's your turn to fall into a mother-in-law's clutches, is it?' she joked.

'What about you?' I asked her. 'Won't you ever go back to yours?'

She guffawed. 'I learnt enough when I was there, Jijji,' she replied. 'There's nothing I care to add to that basic *tiraining*. I won't go back as long the old hag is alive. When I ran away, I swore that I'd rather eat the flesh of a corpse than go back to her cursed house as long as she lived there!'

'What are you doing but eating dead flesh now?' I whispered in her ear. She stuffed her perfumed chador in her mouth and shook with laughter and looked at me as if to say: 'Touche!'

'*Phurst-kilass* joke, Chhoti Jijji!' She saluted me. 'Go on, ask me how many I've devoured by now! All men are our enemies, understand Chhoti Jijji?' She rolled her eyes as she went on softly so that only I would hear her. 'When I see them staring at me, my whole being shudders with anger. Until I have avenged myself on each and every one of them, I will not be able to douse the flames that eat away at me.'

I stepped back as I saw the rage on her face. Then she smiled at everyone and settled down to sing. As I listened to her brilliant performance that evening, I could not help wondering how my childhood friend had turned into such a man-hater. When had a gurgling stream turned into a full-flooded torrent?

Years and years later, while on a visit to Madhya Pradesh, I found myself headed to the annual fair held at Orchha's Kundeswar Mahadev temple. A fan of mine was the local MP, and he insisted that I go there in his car which had a red light and a siren and all kinds of embarrassing accoutrements. Anyway, as I stepped out from that car amidst the gaping villagers, a familiar perfume came dancing to tickle my memory. I looked here and there for her and she came like an arrow, piercing the crowd around the car, and threw herself at my neck. Her eyes were sunk into their sockets but still lined with surma, and although she had hardly any teeth, three beauty spots were still tattooed on that withered chin. I disengaged myself gently from her perfumed chador and asked her softly: 'So how many have you devoured by now, Binnu?'

Her delighted laughter rang over the tents and trinkets and she dragged an old man by the arm to present him to me. 'I've been with him for the last ten years,' she said. 'The old hag died and so I went back,' she said proudly. Then she turned to her husband and said wickedly, 'Ask Chhoti Jijji to tell you what she whispered in my ears just now,' and winked at me. For a brief second, her withered face was transformed into a naughty girl's.

Her old man folded his hands together and bent low to greet me, unable to frame even a word in reply. Binnu snuck up to my ears again and whispered, 'I've been on all the four pilgrimages, Jijji, and even got a dharamsala and a temple constructed. I hawked all the ornaments I had earned from that cursed trade and put the money into constructing that dharamsala and temple. I swear, I don't even have a ring of that sinful pile now. Then, I bathed in the Ganga and washed my past away. Tell me, Chhoti Jijji,' she asked me innocently, 'I am not a sinner any more, am I?'

I had no answer to that disarming question. But I am sure that if my rebellious childhood friend stands one day before the highest throne and turns to ask the Almighty the same question, He will forgive all her sins.

Ama

We have a saying in Kumaon: '*Mai jane mait, bhe jane daij*' – one's parents' home withers after a mother and gifts vanish after the death of a brother. After my mother's death, I went back just once to our home in Almora, and what I saw there was so painful that I could never muster the courage or inclination to ever return. There is so much that I could write about that last visit, but I know I will never be able to bring myself to do it. They say that even the most accomplished surgeon hesitates to wield the scalpel on those he loves the most. Perhaps this is equally true of a wise writer. However, I believe that such surgery is often necessary to preserve the health of others. If a writer honestly shares her life's experiences with her readers, some hidden truths will perhaps be revealed to the reader as well. But after such knowledge, how many of us can detach themselves from a painful truth and accept it with humility? More importantly, how many have the generosity of spirit that asks one to forgive?

As I sit down today to paint a portrait of my mother Ija, I feel overcome with the same emotion that I feel when I offer flowers to a beloved deity. My mother was the strength behind my writing, she was the source that nourished my artistic impulse and gave me the courage to face life with my head held high. Even at the age of eighty-five, her memory was as sharp as a razor. Just a few days before her death, when I asked her to cook me her famous stuffed potatoes, she sent for a small brazier and cooked for me, even though she could hardly move by then. Four days later, she was gone, and I still marvel at the mother's love that made her drag the last ounces of her failing strength to cook a favourite dish for a favourite child.

Can one ever forget such a mother? So, if my portrait of her seems larger than life, let me assure my readers that she was like no other woman I have known. Her life will reveal several episodes that may startle the reader, but none, I know, will bore them.

I was born in Rajkot and, after almost eight decades, I can recall virtually every nook and cranny of that haveli, for its memories are dearer to me than all the riches of the world. Facing our home was the haveli of the Nagars, a wealthy Gujarati Brahmin family. As is often the case with old havelis, both straddled a lane so narrow that we could almost stretch our hands out of one of our windows and touch one on the other side. That window was to become the melting pot of two cultures: Kumaoni and Gujarati. We exchanged our Kumaoni *singal* (pretzel-shaped sweets made of semolina) and our *jambu*-flavoured potatoes with their delicious kokam-flavoured sweet-and-sour Gujarati dal and frothy *khamman dhoklas*; often, pretty Gujarati folk songs wafted over as well and Ija loved to hum them as she went about the house. I remember one:

Aaj to sapna main mane dolna dungar divyajo . . .

I dreamt of the rolling mountains today . . .

Another was:

Janani nu jor, sakhi,
Nahin mere le lale . . .

There is nothing in the whole wide world, my friend,
To compare with one's mother . . .

Still another, which was also sung during the garba dance was:

Mehndi to abe Malwe
Aino rang gayo Gujarat
Mehndi rang lagya . . .

The henna that was brought from Malwa
Has coloured the land of Gujarat . . .

Another devotional song that she often hummed while cooking had obviously touched a deep chord in her heart:

Binukaaj aaj maharaj
Laaj gayi meri
Dukh haro Dwarkanath
Sharan main teri . . .

I lost my modesty
For no particular reason today, my Lord

Spare me my sorrow, O Dwarakanath
I seek the sanctuary of your feet . . .

My mother, whom we called Ija, was to shoulder several tragedies as her life progressed. The first was the death of my sister Chanda and her husband, who left two small infants in her care. Then my father went; a few years later, his brother too and, with them, the days of happiness and plenty. But what shook her to the core was the death of my handsome brother Tribhi, her favourite and most beloved child. What life could never rob her of, though, was her indomitable will to survive with dignity. When my father died suddenly in faraway Bangalore, she was left with nothing but the burden of a large family. My father's friend, Mr Henry, helped us to somehow make our way back to Almora, but what confronted us there was an all-pervading darkness. Not one of her children was married, not one employed. Mr Henry offered her money, but my proud mother politely and firmly turned down his generous handout. She would never, she told us, spread her hands before someone else. We will manage somehow, she vowed before us. The Almighty never shuts all doors together, she was fond of saying, He always leaves a window open somewhere.

This lesson in self-reliance is the first we learnt from our mother: never beg for help; keep giving, but never seek alms. Even if the person who offers you help is your own child, always remember that one day that child will begin to resent your constant alms-seeking. It was a lesson that none of us forgot.

A photograph of my mother, taken just after she was married, used to hang in her father's house and later in Kasoon, our family home in Almora. It is imprinted in my mind so clearly that I can still see her solemn face gazing at the camera. Her tiny frame is almost smothered in a heavy silk sari with a rich gold border and every bit of her is dripping with ornaments – ropes of pearls round her neck, long earrings, bangles and rings.

We never actually saw these historic jewels except in that photograph, for by the time we grew up, Ija had given away every one of them or used them to buy whatever was needed to bring up the family after she was widowed. 'This necklace' – she pointed out a heavy diamond-studded piece in the picture to us gawping children – 'was given by the nawab of Daulatpur when I got married, these bangles by the raja of Gauba . . .'

'But where are they now?' we asked.

'That one I sold to marry off Nan Gusain (an old servant) and build his house, these bangles I hawked when I married Panchi Bai (her Gujarati maid) . . .' She listed the lost treasures without a trace of regret. Like the Statue of Liberty, Ija turned our house a shelter for the homeless and destitute. My father's only brother remained a bachelor all his life. He was strongly attracted to sadhus and spent his life in their company, filling their chillums with marijuana. Once, and only once, did he agree to consider getting married. Perhaps the unusual beauty of the girl drew him out of his shell. However, Pandit Rudra Datt Pant, our family astrologer, came to my grandfather with the two horoscopes. 'How can I allow this, Pandejyu?' He shook his head sadly. 'I have served this family for years, so I cannot hide the truth from you when your son's future is in question. Here, see these horoscopes for yourself. This girl has Mars in her eighth house and he is the Lord of her destiny. It is like receiving a death sentence from the Maker Himself . . .'

So that was that. Never again did our uncle consent to another match, with the result that Ija was the only daughter-in-law that my father's family ever saw.

Ija's father was a well-known surgeon of Lucknow and she was given so much jewellery when she was married that she never wore half of it, she used to say. But that never stopped her from giving it away freely. She told us how, just before she was taken to the chamber where her *kanyadaan* was to be performed, her mother locked her inside a small room in one corner of the house that also doubled up as a sort of larder with sacks of wheat, rice and sugar piled there. 'Don't you dare peep out of the window to see your own wedding procession, Munni,' she was warned by her mother. 'Do that, and be sure that your groom will be a toothless old man!'

So Ija sat down quietly to wait for the time when she would be led down. She was just ten years old then; sitting quietly and not peering out of the window to see a wedding procession (never mind that it was her own) must have been a terrible punishment. Then, she remembered that next to this room, in a tiny hovel, lived a Bengali family. Ija would often, when her mother was not around, give them food stolen from the house. Tomorrow, I will be gone, Ija thought, who will feed these poor people? She knocked softly on the door between the two rooms. No one answered. Apparently, the whole family had gone off to see the wedding procession in the main house. Only the old grandmother, ill with fever, lay there. 'I said nothing,' Ija told us. 'Before they came to fetch me, I quickly pushed over a few sacks of wheat, rice and sugar into the dark hovel, then quickly locked the door and sat down quietly. Thankfully, no one used to count sacks of wheat and rice those days!' She laughed.

All her life, as far back as I can remember, Ija shared whatever her prosperous home had with those less fortunate. She always told us that whatever you give comes back twice over to you: share with one hand and save with the other. Yet, if she ever felt someone was taking advantage of her generosity, she could be equally unforgiving. Once, when she was staying with her granddaughter Madhuri, Madhuri's maid brought a tin of flour to the house. 'It gets so late by the time I reach home, Bahuji,' she told my niece, 'that I have decided to bring over our flour so that I can make chapatis for my family before I leave.' Naturally, no one had any objection. In any case, she was given a decent salary and her midday meal by Madhuri, so what if she wanted to take her son some extra food, Madhuri thought. Then, Ija noticed that while their flour was depleted in no time, the maid's magical tin of flour never seemed to be empty. So one day, when the maid was not around, Ija opened the tin and marked the top with a palm print.

Fifteen days later, when she opened the tin again, the palm print was still there!

Then there was an aunt, a distant relative, whose indolent husband's only gift to her was a child every year. The family had no income and, every other day, this aunt would arrive at our doorstep with her football team. Her sons were wild and kicked up a storm wherever they went, but my mother never said a word. She would quietly send word to the kitchen that they were to add ten more portions to the meals cooked that day. Our old Lohaniji would grumble audibly, but the entire clan was fed nevertheless. Later, wherever she was, whether in Tikamgarh or Rampur, Ija would send huge parcels of food – rice, flour, tea, sugar – along with pullovers for the boys and clothes for the aunt. Years later, I met the aunt, bent and crippled with arthritis now but dressed in good clothes. She hobbled over to meet me and took my hand in her gnarled claw. 'How are the boys?' I asked her. She looked at me with pride as she reeled off how well they were all doing and how comfortable she was now. 'I gave birth to them, child,' she said, 'but it was your mother who fed and clothed them for sixteen years. Boju (my mother) was our Annadata, our benefactress, child – she gave us so much that she must have gone to heaven triumphantly riding a chariot of solid gold!'

I could go on and on, for Ija's army of dependants was famous all over Kumaon.

Among the many people my mother collected around her was a beautiful child-widow called Mohini, who was about my brother Tribhi's age. Mohini, called Munna by all of us, was just ten years old when she was sent back by her husband's family after his death so that she could be looked after by her brothers. Munna's brothers were friends of my father's only brother, a bachelor all his life who later became a hermit. The older one, a handsome rake called Chani Mastan, went hunting one day and never returned. They found his body three days later in the jungles behind Cheena Peak in Nainital. Her second brother, called Dajyu by everyone for his generous nature, was a university teacher. After he died of tuberculosis, my uncle took Munna to Ma Anandamayi's ashram, for how could he, a bachelor, look after a young and beautiful girl? When Ija heard this, she went flying across to the ashram to rescue her. Munna was scheduled to take her vows as a nun the next day and they were preparing to shave off her hair. Ija's heart melted at the sight of this beautiful girl, sitting quietly with her head resting on her knees, and she decided then and there to take Munna back with her and bring her up as her own child.

'How can a girl of her age be forced to forsake the world?' she asked my uncle angrily. 'Munna will stay here and become my tenth child. She will go to Santiniketan with Jayanti and Gaura, and that is that.' So Munna came with us when we went back to Santiniketan that year and became a disciple of Nandalal Bose in Kala Bhavan. Before she left Almora, my mother slipped glass bangles on her wrists, threw out her white widow's weeds and gave her a stack of bright saris to wear. Ija then put a bindi on

Munna's forehead and told her: 'Remember, Munna, if you have a clear conscience, there is no need to fear anyone. Forget what the world will say: why care for people who will talk anyway?'

No one can understand now how radical and subversive this decision was in Almora in those days. For years, a whispering campaign was launched by spiteful people against Ija. People even said that she was grooming Munna to join the nawab of Rampur's harem as my father was the home minister there. Ija stood her ground: she dared anyone to come and say this to her face. No one did.

In one of her last letters to me, Ija wrote: 'I have seen more deaths than I care to remember and God knows how many more I am destined to see . . . The biggest curse of old age is that people hide things from you, assuming that you will not be able to deal with bad news. What rubbish this is! Old age can dim all your senses, but your sixth sense becomes more acute as you grow older. I can hardly see any more, my hearing is not what it was, but my personal warning system alerts me about which of my children is in trouble.

'How are you? What exactly is wrong with you? One last order from me to all of you: none of you are allowed to leave this world before me. I have taken so many knocks that I do not know whether I care to take another . . .'

When I recall the suffering of her last years, I feel as if a macabre game of snakes and ladders had cursed her to come down to '2' after having reached '99'. Perhaps it was this that made Ija treat life as a joke to be laughed away.

Till her death, she kept us amused with her antics and her sharp tongue spared no one. One incident brings out her spirit of resilience most vividly to me.

A few years ago, kerosene oil went underground in Almora, and the grocer who had opened a shop just outside Kasoon promised to send us some. Ija sent him four empty bottles for refilling and waited. Then she was told that the wretch had sent the whole consignment to some officer in town. She sent her servant to ask him what had happened to the promised bottles of kerosene. He was sorry, there was just enough to fill one bottle, he replied, and the servant flashed the solitary bottle in front of Ija's furious face. 'Wait,' she told her servant. She hobbled across to her secret hoard, pulled out two bottles she had stashed away and added a box of matches and wrote a note to the grocer. It read: 'You wretched worm, I am sending you some bottles of kerosene and a box of matches. Pour the oil on your head and set it aflame with my matches. Today is Baikunth ekadasi – I promise you will go straight to heaven.'

PART THREE

Shibi

Her name was not really Shibi. Her uncle, the head priest of the Viswanath Temple next to Almora's cremation grounds, had named her Shivapriya – Shiva's beloved – when she was born. He had chosen the name deliberately, hoping that if her mother (who was his sister) were to call out the Lord's name every day, she may wash away some of her sinful past. But that was not to be. Shibi's mother died within a year of her birth, riddled with a host of vile diseases she had picked up from various lovers.

So little Shivapriya grew up in her uncle's care, running happily all over the modest little hut he lived in. Her uncle was a bachelor, not strange considering his calling. Who, after all, would agree to marry a man who presided over Almora's spooky cremation grounds? Since Viswanath was the town's only burning ghat, never did a day pass without at least one corpse arriving there to complete the end of a journey on earth. As soon as little Shibi heard the funereal chant of '*Ram naam satya hai . . .*' she darted to wake her uncle. 'Quick, get up, Mama,' she'd call out excitedly. 'Here comes another one!' And if her half-stoned uncle refused to rise, she would shake him awake with encouraging remarks: 'Come on, hurry up! I am sure this one's a dead Brahmin, Mama! Just hear how softly they are chanting the *Ram naam*.' Then she'd run to the window and come back clapping her hands: 'The procession has seven gas lamps, Mama! They are bound to have a good shawl as a shroud!' Later, as her uncle presided over the cremation rituals, she stood on the veranda outside the hut to watch the spectacle of the pyre being lit as if it was a fireworks display.

As the embers from the pyre died down, Shibi's home was enveloped in its usual suffocating gloom. Her uncle came back after performing the final rites, often cursing the thoughtless people who died whenever they liked. 'The wretches don't even wait for a decent hour,' he'd grumble. 'Is this any time to drag a man out of a warm bed, I ask you? Look at this milord who decided to cop it at two in the morning! And as if that weren't bad enough, just take a look at the tawdry shroud his father had bought! Who would say that the old Pandeji had come to cremate his twenty-five-year-old son if they saw this cheap shawl he'd covered the body with? Talk of tight-fisted relatives! When your mother died, I had draped a Benarasi dushala over her . . .' And he muttered away like this until, soothed by a puff of marijuana, he fell asleep once more.

But Shibi remained wide awake. She'd pull out a bright pile of shawls from a chest and spread them around her.

This was her treasure and she loved preening herself as she tried them on, one by one. She'd wrap a shawl round her head or wind it round her waist to pretend she was a bride dressing up for a wedding. Eventually, when she tired of this game, she'd gather them together in a pile and burrow into the soft mountain and drift into pleasant dreams. The living and the dead had not registered their difference on her brain yet, nor did thoughts of heaven and hell scare her. She couldn't care less if the fire in her uncle's kitchen was not lit every evening, but if she did not get her daily fix of a funeral pyre, her tiny frame drooped with sadness for having lost out on a shawl for her treasure chest.

Shibi's carefree childhood came to an end when her uncle realized that a cremation ground was not the best place to bring up a young girl. He had a cousin in Nainital and that is where he planned to send her now, even though he thoroughly disapproved of that woman's profession. When he took her there, his cousin's eyes lit up with delight as they fell on the lissom Shibi. The girl was painfully thin and was sure to catch every infection that floated by. As it is, her nose dribbled snot on her upper lip, but still, thought the old aunt, at least she is young and fair. The aunt herself was nothing much to look at, but she was still famous all over Kumaon for her voice and dancing. Under her expert grooming, Shibi gradually blossomed into a very attractive young woman.

Every evening, as the shadows fell, the aunt's house would stir to life. Incense sticks were lit and the aunt and Shibi sat propped on their bolsters, puffing away at their cigarettes as they awaited their clients. One by one these arrived and their court filled up. Among the assembly were some khadi-clad, small-time politicians, a few young drifters from the bridge and card players of Boat House Club and the town's moneylenders, who looted the simple villagers and ran tourist lodges that filled their coffers each summer. Shibi accepted their offerings with the stony-eyed disdain with which temple idols accept offerings made by guilt-ridden devotees.

Finally, after a row with her aunt, Shibi set up her own establishment in a house on the sprawling lands attached to Nainital's Ramsey Hospital. Its gabled tin roof was barely visible among the pear and apple trees that grew all around. Shibi shared the bungalow with a poor Christian family who had sub-let a part of it for a nominal rent to her. They shared a common veranda and this is where she now sat each evening to catch the attention of the young men walking past the house, like the fishermen who sat on the town's lakeside, waiting to snare a fat catch. Few could resist the dark eyes that Shibi shone on them in the gloaming and they flocked to her like bees to a flower.

The Christian family had of a pair of twins: David and Henry, both clerks at the local missionary schools. Their father was the khansama at the local padre's and their mother an ayah at Ramsey Hospital. Neither was married nor would they, sniffed their mother, as long as that witch stayed next door. Shibi was delighted with her new set-up, for the boys would bring her delicious leftovers from the padre's table, purloined by their father for his sons. Her sickly frame filled out and her wilted neck turned upright like the hood of a serpent unfurling. David and Henry also brought her several old English magazines and, even though the print made little sense to her, she copied their fashionable hairstyles and clothes. Sometimes, the twins took her to the local cinema to show her Hollywood films and Shibi allowed them to grope her in the dark as she drank in the glamour of Sophia Loren and Gina Lollobrigida's films. When she came back, she stood in front of the cracked mirror in her tiny bathroom to suck in her cheeks so that she could look like them.

The twins were crazy about her and would have married her as soon as she said yes. They had even worked out an agreement to share her between themselves if she chose one, but Shibi just smiled mysteriously when they proposed. David learnt the latest hit songs and nearly burst his lungs as he whistled them outside her window, but Shibi merely turned enigmatic like Ingrid Bergman or remote like Grace Kelly as she heard his mating calls. When old Colonel Dickory died, David hawked his wristwatch to buy a dressing table from the auction for Shibi, and the twins, huffing and puffing, lugged it to her room; they'd often heard her complain about the tiny mirror she had because she couldn't see all of herself when she got ready. Now, she twirled delightedly before its three piers, turning this way and that to admire herself.

That mirror brought her such good luck that soon her little bedroom could hardly contain the gifts her suitors showered on her. Shibi chose her lovers like a clever prime minister choosing his cabinet. Among them was a rich timber contractor, who gave her carved walnut furniture to offset the dressing table, while another supplied her with bolts of rich silks and chiffons from his shop. One stitched her blouses to perfection, while a goldsmith lover nearly went blind crafting her bracelets and necklaces late into the night. She even had a dhobi lover, who starched her dupattas with shiny mica motes and perfumed them with ittar. There were poets and politicians, surgeons and students . . . In short, Shibi was Kumaon's Christine Keeler and she twirled her lovers like a top.

There was just one among her assembly who could twirl Shibi: Dharnidhar. When he sat next to her, blowing smoke rings into her face with his locks falling over his eyes, Shibi melted like wax. He just had to say 'Darling!' or 'Honey!' to her in his thrilling voice and Shibi could deny him nothing. He once brought her a soft, quilted dressing gown that his father had brought for his mother from one of his foreign jaunts. But his mother was neither sober when her husband bought it nor when her son took it out of her suitcase for his mistress. A dedicated member of the Boat House Club, Dharnidhar's mother spent most evenings there, playing cards and drinking with her rummy group. Shibi twirled and twisted round and round her room to Dharnidhar's guitar and the sounds of the two singing and dancing brought the twins to her window. They peeked in and were so miserable at the sight that they fell upon each other's necks and wept and wept until their rooster came and crowed right next to their legs.

Early next morning, they went across to apologize for their behaviour. Shibi was lying sprawled, drunk on the whisky that she and her lover had shared. She had vomited over herself and the room was stinking. The twins moved her, washed her face, changed her clothes and then brought their cheap talcum powder to kill the stink of the liquor in the room. Finally, Shibi opened her eyes, fixed her red eyes on the two and slurred: 'Get out!' Recalling how they had painstakingly taught her to say that, the twins recoiled at the venom behind the insult.

Shibi's lover came after midnight and vanished like a feral cat before dawn. Catching him was impossible, and despite the twins' best efforts to nab him, he managed to give them the slip each time. The ultimate rebuke was offered to them by Shibi herself. 'Don't you dare hurt him,' she warned them one day. 'If I ever see the two of you skulking around here, I'll fix you!' she threatened and tossed her head.

The twins knew this was no idle threat. Dharnidhar's father was not just a powerful politician, he had also perfected the art of decimating rivals with such finesse that no finger ever be pointed towards him. Dharnidhar was his sole heir and a product of the most expensive education money could buy. His friends called him 'Dicky', for with his fair skin, pink cheeks and romantic curls, he did indeed look more a foreigner than Indian. Dicky's clothes were stitched abroad, and when his hair needed a trim, he went all the way to Delhi, claiming that Nainital's rustic barbers could not be trusted. No one in Nainital could match his skill on the skating rink, and when he turned and twisted expertly with his hands clasped behind his back, the local girls swooned over his dancing limbs. By the time Dicky turned eighteen, he could tell you the vintage of the scotch he was offered after the very first sip. At the time of the annual Fancy Dress Ball in the Boat House Club, he won hands down, and when he dressed once as a wounded soldier the town could not stop talking about it for days. His father's wealth, his mother's clout as a social worker and his own good looks opened every door for him in life. When no Indian university could tempt him to complete his bachelor's degree, his indulgent father sent him abroad. But after he had blown up his allowance on non-scholarly pursuits, Dicky returned home once again with no degree in hand.

His father had thrown up his hands in despair. By now, matters were seriously wrong and his son had given up even caring for himself. All day he lay about in his darkened room, stoned or drunk. His mother – in between knitting woollies for the soldiers in Ladakh and NEFA or packing jams and pickles for them – would try and coax her son to pull himself together. But with half her mind on the brave young men fighting on our borders, she could hardly spare the time for the young man at home. Her mind was clearly elsewhere. Dicky's father Rudradev wept and pleaded with his son, pulled at his grey hair to draw his son's attention to the family's reputation, but nothing worked. He had to accept that an arrow and a wayward son never come back. He first cursed his son in English and when his heart refused to cool he let loose a volley of the choicest abuse in Hindi. When he turned around to confront Dicky, he realized his son had left the room and that his abuses had burnt no ears other than his own. His eyes filled up when he remembered how, in the past, whenever he scolded his son, the little boy would look at him with tearful eyes and say: 'I promise I won't do it again, Papa!' He shook his head and accepted that Dicky's eyes would never again well up with tears of contrition.

Rudradev sat with his head bowed for a long, long time. He could have dealt with his son's drinking – after all, young men do go through these defiant spells – but yesterday, when his friend Gauri Shah had told him about Dicky and Shibi, he had hung his head in shame. Gauri Shah, he knew, was secretly pleased with his friend's humiliation, although he pretended to commiserate with him, and this sharpened his helpless rage. He had heard about Shibi; in fact, he had even seen her once and been quite taken with her. Then, one day, when he saw his wife's dressing gown drying on Shibi's clothesline, he was so upset that he could not find the heart to go to the club for three whole days. Yet, when he broached the subject with his wife, she told him to handle it himself. She was leaving to attend an important women's seminar in Madras, she said busily, and needed to concentrate on preparations for that.

Meanwhile, Shibi's life was thriving. Dicky came early in the evening and stayed on and on. Her other suitors – the dhobi, the goldsmith, the draper – were livid at her for ignoring them so completely and threatened to beat him up for hogging all her attention. But Shibi shrugged off their complaints just as she threw out all her low-type clients from her assemblies and stopped going out anywhere at all. As for David and Henry – they also faded away from her life. David was struck down with tuberculosis and sent off to the Bhowali sanatorium, where his twin nursed him devotedly. Their old father would occasionally wink or whistle at Shibi, but one day, after his wife heard him whistle, she cuffed his ears so hard that he lost all the three teeth in his mouth.

The truth was that Shibi had truly fallen in love with Dicky. She even forgot that, in her profession, she was not allowed to buy lovers – in fact, she was the one up for sale. Meanwhile, Dicky's father was waiting to prise her away from his son; the question was: should he kill the enemy with one stroke or let her slowly bleed to death? Rudradev had two goons in Haldwani – Mehboob and Mahmud – whom he had kept for fixing problems like Shibi. After one signal from him, they abducted Shibi and left her at a remote village on the Nepal border. With Shibi safely out of the way, Rudradev turned his attention to fixing his son. He took him away on long trips to Java and Sumatra when he led a parliamentary delegation to those countries and then came back after a long holiday in the Andaman islands. He had heard that penguins cruelly throw off their young from a cliff to teach them to swim and decided that that is what he would do. Dicky soon learnt to outdo his father in making money: smuggling and hustling his way as he grew. The father found a rich heiress for him, and when Dicky married her, his father donated rupees one lakh to the Prime Minister's Relief Fund. People whispered among themselves that this was hush money he had paid to protect himself from police raids, but charity silences most tongues.

After she disappeared, Shibi's other lovers fell upon bad days: the goldsmith never recovered from the Gold Control Ordinance and the tailor took to selling chaat during summer to the tourists who came to Nainital for cheap holidays. 'Who shall I stitch for now?' he lamented to friends. 'My eyes recognize just one set of measurements.' David had passed on his disease to his twin and both of them now coughed in unison. In short, all of Shibi's lovers seemed to have vanished into the blue.

This time when he returned to the hills from abroad, Rudradev was inundated with requests for inaugurations. He had attended so many by now that his neck ached from the garlands that were hung round it. Today, he had to go to Almora to inaugurate a new women's wing in the Leper Asylum there. He forced a smile as he got out of the car and folded his hands to acknowledge the claps that greeted him. Look at him, they whispered, he doesn't even flinch as he shakes hands with some of the patients! What a man!

He was guided to the new ward, where a blue ribbon awaited the chief guest. He turned to look at the patient who stood with a silver salver and pair of scissors and put out his hand to take it when his eyes fell upon the face. How strange it is, is it not, that fate makes you confront what you wish most to avoid. The colour drained from Rudradev's face, for there, holding the ceremonial salver in her disfigured hands, stood Shibi. How had she reached here, he panicked, perspiring profusely through his Nehru jacket. Had she picked up the disease in Nepal then and arrived here for treatment? His whole body shook uncontrollably as he picked the scissors and cut the ribbon. He put the scissors back and avoided meeting her eyes because he must not give anything away. Then he swiftly moved on, terrified that she would say something, but she did not. Shibi said nothing and looked at him without blinking. Her face was now a hideous mockery of what it once was. The rosy skin of her youth had hardened with leprosy to become the gnarled hide of a jackfruit. Her silky eyelashes had fallen off so that her eyes looked perpetually wide open. Rudradev felt them bore holes into his back.

Then, suddenly, out of nowhere, an angelic-looking girl came and stood next to her, holding one of Shibi's stubby fingers. She stared at Rudradev with her clear blue eyes, arresting him right there. There was no place for doubt: those blue eyes were his family's signature feature and for four generations they had been handed down from father to child. Shibi's little daughter was the asylum's plaything. Even Rudradev stumbled towards her, then halted and then turned on his heels and walked swiftly away. He fumbled for his wallet, but when he opened it, there were just two denominations of notes there: hundred- and one-rupee ones. His fingers hovered over one and then the other, but those blue eyes haunted him. Finally, he wrenched out a hundred-rupee note, handed it to the child and almost ran to his waiting car, leaving behind him whispering lepers amazed at this generous donation.

Not once did he dare to look back as he hurriedly bade goodbye to the doctors and nurses assembled to see him off.

As his car drove through the rhododendron, pine and oak trees that lined the drive of the asylum, he tried to steady his nerves. The minute his car drove out of the gates, Rudradev collapsed with relief on the leather seat and shut his eyes. The child's face swam in front of his closed eyelids and he shook his head to clear it.

I could not have forgiven myself if I had handed her a one-rupee note, he said to himself, but why did I give a hundred rupees to that woman's bastard? The next time I go out, he swore, I must put some ten- and five-rupee notes in my wallet as well. Had I thought of it today, would I have given away a hundred rupees to Shibi's whelp?

Dhuan

The day Rajula was born in Nek, a village situated at the edge of Ramgarh, the surrounding hills reverberated with joyous drumbeats and the notes of the local horn, the tuturi. Nek village is still around, but the gappy holes in its dilapidated houses now remind one of the broken teeth in the mouth of an old man; what appears now to be a quaint mockery of the Dalai Lama's fabled Potala Palace in Lhasa was once Kumaon's most famous brothel. Its timber-lined rooms resounded with the jingle of anklets and the beat of the tabla as doe-eyed beauties ran up and down its floors. Their tinkling laughter and lissom bodies drew young men from the neighbouring region here every evening. Among these swains, you could find highborn, long-nosed Brahmins, scions of the most famous Rajput clans and the prosperous moneylenders and bankers of Kumaon. All of them forgot their caste and clan as they vied for the favours of the beauties who lived here in those days. Heaven alone knows, we heard our elders say in shocked tones, how many Pant, Pande and Joshi boys were ruined by those women.

There was something about the very air of the region around Ramgarh, it was said, that intoxicated men, redolent as it was with the heady aroma of apples. In fact, Ramgarh was then less famous for its apple orchards than for the sirens in the village of Nek. There was nothing low or vulgar about their trade, for they believed they would invite divine retribution if they broke their holy vows. They offered you their song and dance as if they were making an offering to the gods, and their music celebrated divine, never-temporal love. No client ever dared to ask them to sing a ghazal or a thumri-dadra, for they sang only devotional poetry set to pure classical ragas. Their broad, serene brows were modestly covered by their veils and as their gaze moved from face to face, it was said, a hushed silence fell upon the listeners. They started their recital with a devotional hymn and ended with the lilting folk song of Kumaon, the *Pari Chanchari*. At the end of the concert, they followed their elders out of the hall with lowered gaze to disappear into one of the surrounding chambers, we had heard.

This is why the birth of a daughter was an occasion of unprecedented joy in Nek village. And when their most famous member, Motiya, was seen sucking a sour lime, she was immediately surrounded by the others.

'It is a daughter this time, I swear,' said Dhana. 'That is why she is asking for sour things, mark my words.'

'I agree,' chirped Pirma. 'Do you think she would have looked so rosy if there was a boy in her womb?'

A huge fuss was made of Motiya after that day. Thirty-two hearts fluttered in expectation when she went into labour. Their family tree was in danger of drying up because the last birth, fifteen years ago, had been Chandra's son. This is why, the day Rajula was born, their whole community danced and sang and hugged each other in joy. Some men were immediately dispatched to Nainital to fetch the Gurkha band while three halwais set up enormous vats to fry sweets and savouries for the whole village. Separate, pure food was cooked for the Brahmins in pure ghee and three fat sheep were roasted on a pit nearby for the Rajputs. Rajula's 'aunts', draped in their polka-dotted rangvali veils, went from house to house to invite the guests, and God knows how long it took for the young men to recover from those smiles and coy invitations!

At her naming ceremony, the pandit blushed as he whispered her name into the baby's little ears through a conch shell. 'Your name is Rajula, or Rajeshwari, or Radhika,' he declared and then looked deeply embarrassed. 'This is actually the privilege of the child's father,' he told the assembly.

'So what, Panditjyu,' he was told. 'This child is definitely someone from your own caste.' They giggled. 'Just look at her colour!'

The poor man smiled weakly. Handing him a hefty amount, the eldest of Rajula's aunts silenced his doubts with such an enchanting look that the poor man was lost. 'I cast her horoscope last night,' he told her, shaking his head in wonder. 'What stars this child has been blessed with! She has the *ratnanjali yoga*, Pirma, a rare configuration that only kings and princes are born with! Her palms will always be filled with precious stones.' He went on, describing the astrological wonder by cupping his own hands to indicate its scope. 'Understand? Ratnajanli yoga,' he muttered to himself, shaking his head as if he could not quite believe what he had seen.

'Oh, come on, Panditjyu,' Pirma teased him. 'I am sure we all have the same yoga,' she joked, and burst into a peal of tinkling laughter as the poor man blushed yet again.

Rajula assuaged the maternal longings of thirty-two breasts. Like a fish that slithers from hand to hand before slipping back into the lake, Rajula was passed from aunt to aunt. This is exactly how Rajula's own mother, Motiya, had been brought up. Long ago, tired of the cruelties she'd endured at the hands of her mother-in-law, Motiya's mother had shaved her hair, donned saffron robes and gone off to spend the rest of her days at the feet of a Nepali baba at his ashram. Heaven knows what brought her to Nek village and take to this life. Life had shown her every kind of pain and joy here: she had seen her eldest daughter die a wretched death at the young age of twenty-two, her body covered with syphilitic sores. She had sworn she would never give birth to another daughter, but that vow was made to be broken, and Motiya was the result of that breach.

As Motiya grew older, her line of suitors grew longer by the month. 'The older the honey, the sweeter it is,' Motiya was told by her mother. 'Motiya, you are the jewel in our crown.' Each year, before the famous procession of the Nanda Devi temple took place, Motiya was summoned by the temple authorities to dance in front of the holy palanquin. Decked in a velvet ghaghra, with a perfumed silk handkerchief in her hand, the dancing Motiya was followed by crowds of eager young men. No wedding procession of a noble house could start before Motiya had danced before it, decked in gold from head to foot.

When Rajula turned eight, she was initiated into the arts of music and dance by her adoring aunts. A goat was sacrificed and Ustad Bundu Khan inscribed an 'Om' on Rajula's little red tongue. A few days later, when he taught her a snatch of Bhairavi, she copied it so effortlessly that the ustad's eyes shone. 'My dear child, *you* should be my ustad now,' he joked. 'Motiya, my dear, this is a rare diamond – look after her well. Mark my words, one day she will be a greater performer than all of you put together. Send her to the plains, I beseech you, don't let her languish here.'

'The plains?' her mother replied in horror. 'Where the hot loo will burn the roses on her cheeks?' Rajula's aunts wilted at the dreaded prospect of their flower being singed by such heat, but Bundu Mian was not to be dissuaded: he knew a jewel when he saw one. This child was destined for greater things, he told the aunts, they would be foolish to hold her back. Bundu Mian had a sister who lived in Lucknow and ran a well-known establishment there. She entertained only select clients and accepted invitations only from the most aristocratic families. 'Do you know,'

Bundu Khan told Rajula's simple aunts, 'gramophone companies pay her a fortune to record her *Raga Megh*? What would you all know of such sophisticated singing, hain? All you can manage is some devotional songs and folk songs. Have you ever heard a real ustad perform? I have seen Benazir reduce a renowned tabla player to a sweating mass of blubber as she teased him with an unending taan. The poor man fell at her feet when she finally came to the *sam*!'

He looked around for the effect of this picture on the simple women and was pleased with the result when he saw eyes widened in fascination.

'All right, you win,' Motiya finally conceded. 'I'll send Rajula to Lucknow with you, ustadjyu. Far be it from me to hold her back.'

So, one day, Ustad Bundu Khan took little Rajula to Lucknow and gave her to his sister Benazir, who immediately locked her up for safe custody. Poor Rajula felt like a nightingale trapped in a golden cage. Gone were the simple joys of running free in the village orchards; in their place was the strict regimen of Benazir's serious, classical education. The loving aunts became a distant memory as one stern look from this new, terrifying aunt dried up her throat.

'Will you never let me go and visit my mother?' she dared to ask her jailor one day, with tears in her eyes.

'You had better learn, you foolish child,' she was told, 'that we have no father or mother. Our profession is our mother and our talent our father, understand? And don't ever come to me with tears in your eyes again!'

Rajula quickly wiped her tears away.

Every morning, three maids would massage her body with sandalwood paste. Then, after a fortifying breakfast of a halwa made of ground almonds and pure ghee, she was sent to the music room, where an eagle-eyed Benazir would supervise her lessons. Slowly and with care, she initiated Rajula into the intricate world of ragas such as *Jaunpuri*, *Malgunji*, *Sohana*, *Lalit*, *Paraj* and *Hindol*, and as Rajula negotiated the difficult path, the faces of her past began to recede from her life. Letters she wrote to her mother never brought back any answers, for God knows whether they were ever sent. Gradually, Rajula could hardly even recall her childhood in the village, let alone her loving aunts and mother.

By the time she turned sixteen, Rajula was a sight to behold. Her slim calves clad in silken churidars were a marvellous vision and her silk kurtas gleamed with diamond buttons. All this could never dim the radiance of her innocent face, which had magically preserved the pastoral innocence of that little village in Kumaon. She was not rounded but slim and lissom and her eyes, though not exceptionally large, had a dense curtain of eyelashes that looked like a swarm of butterflies hovering over a flower. The dainty grace of her high cheekbones was offset by an equally dainty nose. Ethereal and innocent, Rajula was unlike anything that Benazir had handled so far, and this is why she was hidden from the male gaze under layers of cotton wool. Rajula was her Kohinoor, Benazir knew, and she was not prepared to lose it before she had evaluated its worth. Yet, although Rajula feared and respected Benazir, there was little love in her life now. In fact, she would cheerfully run away if ever she got a chance.

Next to Benazir's haveli was another one that belonged to Seth Dadumal, and right in front of Rajula's room – separated by what seemed just a few inches – was the room of Dadumal's son, known as Chhote Seth. After a long spell in his native Marwar, the seth had returned recently to marry off his son to a rich heiress. It was said that her father had given the seth's family a huge dowry to compensate for his ungainly daughter. One day, when the blue curtain of the seth's room was drawn, Rajula chanced upon a sight that made her giggle. With a crumpled sari hitched over her hairy legs, the younger seth's bride was seated on the floor, and lying on one fat thigh was her husband, his face turned away from Rajula as his bride dropped oil in his ear. The sound of Rajula's muffled giggle must have reached across, for the young man sprang up and shut the window with an angry snap. So this was Seth Dadumal's son, Rajula realized. His father was a regular in Benazir's court and it was rumoured that he had gifted Benazir the haveli she lived in. The seth's wife had died when his son was an infant, so the young child was sent off to his maternal grandparents to be brought up. This is why no one had seen him until his wedding. 'Poor Seth Kaka,' Rajula said to herself. 'But perhaps I should pity the son more for being saddled with such an ugly wife.'

Rajula could not get the picture of his handsome body clad in just a crisp dhoti out of her mind. His torso had rippled with taut muscles and a gold chain glistened round his neck, she recalled. Any other man who wore a gold chain round his neck may have appeared effeminate, but the young seth looked like a god, she sighed to herself. Having grown up in a household of women, Rajula's first glimpse of a man with hair on his chest made a deep impression: she looked at her tiny palms and wondered what it would feel like to run them over that chest. Try as she might, she could not put the young seth out of her mind and he often came to haunt her dreams.

After that, she made sure that he saw her properly. So she deliberately chose to plait her long hair near the window that faced his room, or bite into a juicy orange with her red lips so that the juice squirted down her pointed chin. Benazir had tutored her well on how to tease a man and Rajula made full use of her wiles. The young seth didn't stand a chance. On one hand was his spectacularly ugly wife, while across the street, a few inches away, lived the most beautiful girl he had ever seen – so Rajula won the game effortlessly. She would offer him a slice of her orange silently and her eyes would ask: 'Do you want some?' When he came near the window to catch it, she would pop it into her mouth, stick out a saucy thumb and snap her window shut. She could hear him cough, splutter or hum to catch her attention. Then, when the energy emanating from the other window became unbearable, she would slowly open her window, sweep him a come-hither look and disappear once again. This game of love went on, hidden from the jealous eyes of the seth's wife and Benazir's spies.

Each time she opened the window, the young seth felt as if the moon had come out from behind the clouds for him. As for Rajula, her beauty acquired the ripeness and glow that Benazir's unguents and secret cosmetic recipes had failed to achieve. Her cheeks turned pink, her eyes glowed and her ripe lips invited someone to crush them with kisses.

Then, one day, a famous circus came to town. Benazir bought tickets for her household and took them there in a phaeton with curtained windows, for not even a bird could leave her haveli without the purdah in place. In those days, even the courtesans of the Chowk followed the modesty of noble houses and their women were kept in strict purdah. In fact, these establishments preserved the courtly traditions so well that young girls from noble families were sent there to refine their social graces. Their bodies were always covered so that no flesh was ever immodestly displayed. So, Benazir herself supervised Rajula's hair and clothes that day. Her long hair was braided in such a way that her high cheekbones and large eyes were highlighted. Instead of a churidar, she was made to wear a sixteen-yard lehenga that drew attention to her dainty pink feet adorned with silver anklets. Heavy kundan earrings dangled from her ears and around her neck hung a Kumaoni kundan champakali. Benazir knew that many of the town's high families would come there. A ripple would go through that assembly to find out who this beauty was. Today, she would display her Kohinoor for the first time.

As soon as her party entered the marquee, people forgot

to watch the antics of the cycling bear, the lion jumping through a hoop and the glittering trapeze girls. Their eyes were fixed on the ravishing spectacle of Rajula.

Rajula had never seen a circus in her life and her pleasure at the silly, clownish acts of the joker was a sight to behold. She clung in terror to Benazir's arm when the lion roared and scores of young men were ready to leap up and kill the beast.

Among the spectators that day was the young seth and his ugly wife, and his entire attention was centred on Rajula rather than the performers in the ring. Rajula saw this too and smiled mysteriously once before she turned her attention to the stage. That night, when he peeped across the street from his window, Rajula's casement was shut. He sighed and returned to lie next to his wife, and when her huge belly began to reverberate with snores, he sneaked across once more. There was a faint blue light burning in Rajula's room and he stood transfixed at the sight of Rajula humming to herself as she disrobed. His heart began to beat like a pair of bellows as he looked at her rounded arms, her swan-like neck and the gentle swell of her breasts beneath her clothes. He pushed his curtain aside, and the sound made Rajula realize she was being watched. She blushed to the roots of her hair and made to shut the window when something in his eyes stilled her hand.

'You are a very ill-mannered man.' She tilted her chin at him. 'What is your name?'

'Why? Are you planning to report me to the police?

Then be sure to tell them that even if they threaten to hang me from the gallows, I won't stop staring at you.' He hung half his torso out of the window to mime a hanged man and Rajula's hands went up to her mouth to silence her scream. 'Stop!' she called out. 'Please don't go further than that. You might fall down on the street below!'

'What do you care? Do you know how many nights I've spent hanging like this?' He now squatted on the narrow ledge of the window and dangled his legs over the wall. Just a yard or two separated his window from Rajula's, but between the two was a sheer abyss that led straight to the cobbled street below.

She leant out of her window, balancing her hands on the narrow ledge outside that she had constructed for her doves, and smiled at him.

'So what do they call you at home, Chhote Seth?' she asked saucily.

'Lalchand,' he replied. 'And what do they call you?'

'Stop pretending you don't know my name,' she flirted.

'All I know is that your Ammi calls you Rajji,' he said. 'Why don't you come over to our house one day?' he asked.

'You must be out of your mind!' Rajula laughed. 'And have your wife chase me out with a broom? Why don't you come over instead to ours?'

'Are you serious?' he asked throatily. 'Shall I jump across right now?'

'As if you can do that!' she scoffed. 'If you miss your step, you know what will happen, don't you?'

She had barely finished her sentence when he leapt across and almost landed on her. Rajula's face went white with fear. If this madman had fallen, what would she have done? Lalchand took one look at her face and laughed. 'Wasn't that better than those trapeze artists we saw at the circus?'

'Sshh! Not so loud,' she shushed him. 'If Ammi gets wind of this, she'll feed you to the dogs! My god! A man in my room at night?' Her eyes filled up with fear.

'If you say so, I'll leave now,' he said and made to leave, but Rajula caught hold of his hands. That touch sent a current through both and she shut her eyes in ecstasy as she felt a man's touch for the first time in her life. Lalchand clasped her close. 'Do you know how long I've longed for you, Rajji?' he asked her. 'I've pressed my ears to my window to hear you sing and when you plaited your hair or put surma in your eyes, I've flinched with each movement of your hands.'

'Stop!' she cried. She trembled like a leaf with excitement and fear, melted like a snowflake in his arms.

She pushed him away when he tried to kiss her and Lalchand let her go. 'All right, I'll leave now, Rajji,' he said. 'But remember, I'll be back again tomorrow.' Then he kissed her hands in farewell and stood on her ledge.

'Please don't jump,' she pleaded, but with one last loving look at her, he picked up his dhoti and leapt across. The next thing she knew, he was smiling at her from his window across the street.

After that, there was no stopping her leaping lover: rain,

hail, storm or wind, he became bolder and bolder each day. That summer, his wife left to visit her parents for three months and the two lovers were overjoyed. They cooed and billed like a pair of mating doves. They teased and played dangerous games. Often, she would hide and he would look frantically for her before she appeared. Rajula played with him as a cat plays with a mouse.

'What if your Ammi finds out?' he asked her one day as she lay across his lap.

'I'll tell her this thief entered my room and threatened me with a knife to keep silent. He wanted me to tell him where the keys were kept,' she joked.

'What an accomplished liar you are,' he said. 'After all, that is what you are best at, aren't you?' he teased her and she wilted at the cruel reference to her profession. Contrite, her lover spent hours trying to make her smile and forgive him. For three blissful months, they spent all their nights in each other's arms. Often, they woke guiltily at dawn as the muezzin called the faithful to prayer and Lalchand quickly leapt home.

'Tomorrow, your Ammi is going to Malihabad,' he told her. 'I'll come at seven in the evening, Rajji.'

But that evening never came. For once, the accomplished acrobat lost his step. He slipped at her ledge and went plunging down to the cobbled street below. A heartrending scream broke from both as he went down and Rajula was ready to leap down when Benazir herself rushed in to see what had happened.

'I knew it!' she hissed through clenched teeth and pulled

Rajula back into the room. 'I knew someone came to your room because I could smell a man on you. Serves you right, you slut! Allah has punished the sinner and saved me the trouble of dealing with him.'

Rajula spun upon Benazir like a bloodthirsty tigress, but Benazir felled her with one blow. Then she locked her in and strode off. The wails from the seth's haveli came floating across to Rajula, but she could not join the mourners. On the fifth night, she opened her window and peeped across: the seth's room was plunged in darkness. As she looked away, her eyes fell on her ledge where the skid marks of his feet were still imprinted on the dust. She fell upon them and kissed them madly and ran sobbing across the room. That day, the Pathan doorman who brought her meals up each day had probably been too drugged on opium to remember to lock her door. Rajula beat her head against it and it swung open. She hurtled down the steps and fled. When Benazir came up the next morning, she was shocked to see Rajula's door ajar. She pulled her hair, beat her chest and screamed at the world, but Rajula was nowhere to be found. Benazir had lost her Kohinoor.

The night she fled, Rajula could think of no other sanctuary than the village where she had been born. By the time she reached Nek, her lips were cracked and her heels sore, and anyone who saw her matted hair would never recognize the girl she once was. As she stumbled into her old home, she came face to face with an old chowkidar. 'What happened to the women who used to stay here?' she asked. 'Have they gone away?'

The old man opened his sleepy eyes. 'God knows where the whores went.' He spat in disgust. 'You've ruined my ekadasi fast by mentioning them early in the morning. If you had to take the names of some women, why couldn't you have thought of some decent ones? Must have died,' he muttered. 'Who cares? Anything else?'

Rajula stepped back at the venom in his tone. Then she saw the mark of Vishnu on his forehead. 'Forgive me, Maharaj,' she replied politely. 'That was all I needed to ask. What else is there to ask if they are dead anyway?' She sighed.

'Look, lass, I won't start the day with a lie,' the old man said less harshly. 'All of them did not die: three survived – Debuli, Pirma and Dhana. I believe they live in Gagar in some Nepali baba's ashram. Calls himself a baba, the wretch, but all his life he has lived with whores. He has managed to collect three for his old age, and looks like a fourth is ready to join that gang now.'

With this, he spat once more, turned his back and went back to his prayer beads.

She slithered down the steep paths that led to the Nepali baba's ashram. He was her mother's father, she knew, but would be accept her? She would spend the rest of her life at his feet if he did, she resolved.

Rajula entered the cave, filled with the smoke swirling from his dhuni. The minute they saw her, everyone knew who she was: she was the spitting image of Motiya. Old Debuli was blind now, but she caressed Rajula's face with her fingers. Pirma was no longer the beauty she was and

Dhana Mausi remembered every incident from Rajula's childhood. The baba was a Gorakhpanthi, an order recognizable by their hanging earlobes from which dangled large hoops. Rajula resolutely put aside the memories of the jewels her ears had once worn and begged him to pierce her ears with the hoops that would drag her lobes down to her shoulders.

She spent her days now tending to the dhuni, cooking the prasad and looking after the old aunts and the baba. Once in a while, a wandering band of mendicants would come calling and each evening they would take out their cymbals and clappers and sing songs in the dark, smoky cave.

One day, when some sadhus finished their singing, the Nepali baba asked Rajula: 'Why don't you sing for us, my child? I'm told that you have learnt from the great ustads of Lucknow – surely you know a few devotional songs for us?'

Rajula's eyes filled up. She remembered someone telling her how he used to press his ears against his window to hear her sing. God knows how many times she had sung for him in her room when they were alone! On the last night they spent together, he had begged her to sing '*Chale jaiyyo, bedarda, main royi chali jaaon . . .*' for him and she had refused. 'I don't feel like singing that today.' And when he went on, she told him: 'I'm not running away anywhere. I promise I'll sing it another day.'

Only, she hadn't run away – he had. Who was left for her to sing for now?

'Child?' Baba prodded her. 'Won't you sing for us then?'

Rajula sat staring at the flames of the dhuni, somewhere very far away. 'I don't know how to sing, Baba,' she lied and bent over the fire to coax flames out of the wet logs.

'Arre, Ram-ram, what a lot of smoke,' the baba said. 'Your eyes have started watering. Come on, Pirma, you go and take over. This poor child's eyes are streaming red with the smoke.'

Pirma gave a wan smile to Rajula as she pushed her away from the dhuni. She did not know the history behind Rajula's tears, but this she knew for a fact: her eyes were not watering because of the smoke from the dhuni.

This smoke I can deal with, thought Pirma sadly, but how can I ever blow life into the embers burning in that child's breast?

Tope

I've known 'Tope' since the historic time when she really spewed fire and brimstone, like the cannon she was named after. Her small two-storeyed house stood behind ours and you could stretch your hands through the iron railings of our back veranda to touch the roof of her modest home. A creeper of wild flowers covered that roof and often Tope would walk across it, banging nails into the rotting tin sheets to hold them together. In fact, one of the supporting walls once collapsed under her weight, but when she was served a notice from the local municipality to demolish the house as it had become unsafe, Tope stood on her roof, chest puffed out defiantly, and let forth such a volley of abuse against the Hindu municipal chairman that the demolition squad slunk away, never to return.

During the Second World War, a battalion of Australian soldiers was stationed in the small cantonment at Almora. After their arrival, no daughter or daughter-in-law in the town was allowed to go to the temple, leave alone visit the bazaar, and when the soldiers marched through the town, wearing huge hats, their hob-nailed boots crunching the tarmac, shutters and windows were quickly clapped shut in case those red-faced giants caught a glimpse of the pretty faces behind them.

The only window that refused to close its shutters to the bold stares of the Australian giants was Tope's. As soon as she heard the clip-clop of their boots, she'd drape herself at her window to smile and wave at them. Soon, one heard greetings such as 'Hi, honey!' and 'Hi, sweetheart!' along with appreciative whistles and guffaws as Tope kissed her fingers to send across flying kisses to them. We used to be aghast at her boldness for, in those days, even the men in our town were scared of speaking to those red-faced baboons. I never understood how Tope could dare to make such friendly gestures, but then I was too young to see the larger game being played in front of my eyes.

Every evening, as the shadows fell over the town, Tope's courtyard filled up as the Australians came calling. We'd peep from our back veranda and see them, their bare chests covered with lewd tattoos, singing drunken songs and tossing Tope like a rubber ball up in the air as she screamed with delight. This revelry went on till late in the night and sounds of their *ha-ha, hee-hee* floated across to our home. The next morning, if our mother caught sight of her, she would shout across: 'Your father, Thomas Master, lived here for years. And as long as he stayed in this Hindu neighbourhood, he respected our way of life. He'd light diyas at Diwali and played with abeer-gulal during Holi like the rest of us. But look at you! Shameless hussy!'

'But, Ammaji,' my saucy younger bhabhi piped up, 'Tope is playing with colour too! Why are you shouting at the poor thing?' At this, all my three bhabhis would burst into peals of laughter and Tope would join in as well as my mother stomped off, muttering under her breath. I watched them wide-eyed, unable to fathom the double entendres being tossed around. All I knew was that when one of us had once sprayed Tope with some coloured water at Holi, she had almost skinned us alive. Only much later was I able to understand what my bhabhi had meant that day: that Tope had her own secret supply of colour tucked away in her bosom and that, for her, every day was a joyous celebration.

Tope's official name was Christina Victoria Thomas. She was almost six feet tall and her manly figure went well with her rich, deep contralto. This is perhaps why one of the town's wits had named her Tope, or cannon. Yet, like most fat women, Tope was actually a simple, uncomplicated person. She had never cared for female company because when she was a child her schoolteacher father was posted in the remote town of Pithoragarh. Her schoolmates were all boys, most of them tough Bhutias from the nomadic tribes that lived on the Indo-Tibet border near the town. Tope grew up with them, almost like a boy. Then, at some point, a missionary mem spirited her away to Madras, which is where her skin acquired its rich mahogany gloss.

'Tope,' my pretty, pink-and-white bhabhi once asked

her. 'How come you are you so dark? I swear even our domnis are not so black!' I was taken aback at bhabhi's lack of tact, but Tope was impervious to such insults. 'Because I lived in Madras, Bojyu,' she replied. 'Did you know that even the crows are black there?'

After the missionary mem passed away, Tope returned to the hills and was soon declared our little town's scarlet woman. She flaunted her bright clothes and whenever she sailed out in her favourite red sari, my younger bhabhi would taunt her loudly: 'Oh my! Has the coal shed caught fire again?'

Tope would flash her white teeth in reply and push a bright yellow flower into her hair, saying: 'What to do, Bojyu? I'm sick of wearing those drab khaki fatigues every day.'

By now, Tope had joined the Women's Auxiliary Wing of the Army and when she came over to show her new khaki uniform to us, my three bhabhis doubled over with laughter. 'What on earth do you do in the army, Tope?' they asked, giggling helplessly at the sight of her bursting uniform. The youngest bhabhi then whispered something in her ears and Tope flounced off, saying: 'I don't like such cheap jokes!' After that, she never visited our house again.

Three days later, she was sent off to Secunderabad and, on my way to school, I saw her marching in her uniform to the bus stand, behind a coolie carrying her luggage. Then, for several years, no one knew where she was. Meanwhile, my elder bhabhi developed gangrene after a nail pierced her foot and died. The middle one, who came from a family of depressive maniacs, had to be sent off to the mental asylum in Bareilly and the youngest one was bitten by a snake. She survived, but her foot used to swell up like a balloon, making her scream with pain. I often gazed at Tope's abandoned home, now almost a ruin, my eyes filling up as I remembered the good-natured ribbing that once livened our common home boundaries. All my fun-loving bhabhis were gone and, as for Tope, god knows who must now be laughing at her jokes. I hated coming home now.

My husband's job took him on tours to far-off places in the remote valleys of Munsiyari and Garbyang while I was left alone at home. Our children were in boarding schools, so whenever he went on one of these long tours, I'd take off as well. One of my favourite haunts was Mukteshwar, with its neat bungalows, serene mountains and gurgling springs. Often, as I drove across the winding hills and dales to visit my sister who lived there, I came across gangs of workmen singing lilting folk tunes as they worked to repair roads damaged by the rains and landslides. There were some wonderful teashops along the route, where you got tangy yellow raita with mustard that tingled your sinuses and golden-yellow potato gutkas tempered with the Tibetan herb, jambu.

I was travelling to Mukteshwar one day in the monsoon month of Shravan, the time of year when hill women go to worship at the Gufa Mahadev, a famous Shiva temple inside a cave in the region. That day, our bus was full of local village women, resplendent in their bright lehengas and polka-dotted dupattas, with huge gold nose-rings covering half their face. The sonorous sounds of a *Rudri Path* floated up to our ears and an elderly man sitting next to me, prompted by the shameless billing and cooing of a young Punjabi couple in front of us, started a monologue addressed to no one in particular.

'Say what you will, but if there is any modesty left in the world, you will find it in our Kumaon! Come the first Monday of Shravan, and what do you see? Lines of villagers going to bathe the local Shivling with water. Every mountain seems to reverberate with your name, Bhole Shankar, every mountain! Aha-ha-ha!' He closed his eyes in reverence. 'Have you ever seen any vulgar graffiti on our walls? No sir! If there are any advertisements painted on our mountainsides, they say: "Quit tea!" or "Quit drinking!" But go to the plains, and what do you see?' he went on. 'Every wall urges you to get yourself cured of some disgusting sexual disease! *Chhi! Thhu!*' And here he spat out of the window in disgust. Whether it was his faulty aim or the wind's playfulness, I cannot say, but that spit sprayed the young couple in front, and then erupted such a to-do that all of us could not help listening as they really let the old man have it.

By now, the skies had darkened and, with a roll of thunder, down came the rain. It had been raining on and off for the last three days and when the atmosphere inside the bus became too hot, Nature decided to send a shower of cool rain. Suddenly, with an ominous rumble, a huge slice of the mountainside along the road slithered down and the driver braked to avoid ramming into the rubble. He watched helplessly as the stones and mud fell on the road and finally declared he could go no further.

'If you can trust me with your luggage, leave it here and go to Bhowali to spend the night,' he suggested. 'Perhaps you may be able to get some transport from there by tomorrow.'

One by one, all the passengers alighted, carrying a bag of essentials. None of us doubted the honesty of the driver, for all hill drivers are famous for their integrity. It was still raining, but fortunately, I had a raincoat with me, so I covered myself well and started to walk briskly towards Bhowali along a familiar shortcut. I had a widowed niece who worked as the principal of a girls' school there and I decided to spend a few days with her before I returned to Nainital.

As I passed the familiar gates of the Bhowali Sanatorium, my steps faltered as several dear faces floated up from memory. I could see my old childhood friend Kusumi, sitting on the chair near the gates, her pale face ravaged by tuberculosis. Then I remembered my uncle, Tauji, waiting to be carried up on a litter, staring at me in silent goodbye. I can still see his moist eyes, his funny monkey-cap framing a face that we would perhaps never see again. Kusumi died, as did Tauji, victims of a disease that was then considered incurable.

God knows how many have rested in that airy room at the gates before climbing the steep slope to the sanatorium above and then to their final resting place beyond. Across the road was a new rest house, built by the Forest Department for relatives who came to visit their dear ones. As I stood there, lost in my memories, a jeep went swishing past me and stopped a few feet ahead. Out stepped a woman, a bright purple scarf over her hair, her full body encased in tight red jeans and a black cardigan, carrying apples and eggs in both her hands. She turned to say something to the driver that sounded like: 'Give my salaams to your sahib. Tell him I'll send the sputum samples of the three patients tomorrow.' And the jeep drove off.

She hadn't noticed me till now. Then she saw me, standing under the dripping branches of a tree, and walked over. 'Are you looking for someone's house? Can I help you?' she asked, smiling at me. She was out of breath and I watched in fascination as her huge breasts went up and down with each breath she took. Obviously, she hadn't recognized me. How could she? She had last seen me when I was wearing a frock, and now even my daughters had outgrown that stage. I may have changed, but Tope had not. She still had a generous frill of chins, which melted effortlessly into the vastness of her bosom, like so many rivers flowing into the sea. She wore even heavier make-up now and her scarlet lips were a Cupid's bow over a string of false pearls on what must have once been her neck. Her chest still came three steps ahead of the rest of her body to greet you. Her strong perfume tickled my nostrils and spread its fragrance through the area around her and I remembered my youngest bhabhi saying: 'This Tope smells like a bar of English soap.'

'Whose house are you looking for, honey?' she asked again and put down her baskets to wipe the moisture from her face with a handkerchief.

I decided to stop playing games. 'You haven't recognized me, have you, Tope? Look at me again!' I said, laughing as I put my face closer to hers.

'Oh my god!' She started bombarding me with questions. 'You! Here? So grown up! Married and all! What did you say? That your daughters are in the university now? O Mother Miriam, how time flies! Where is so-and-so? How many children does that one have? Did you say that Suriya has two?' She went on and on. 'Looks like all of you have made your own nests. I seem to be the only odd person out, as always! I earn so much, child, that I can't even begin to tell you, but ask me where it goes and I can't say. Come along, I won't allow you to go anywhere but to my cottage. Come!' she ordered, and I had to obey. She chatted away, showering me with hundreds of questions, as we wound our way to her cottage.

Seven tall trees surrounded her cottage, appropriately named 'Seven Oaks'. Beyond them were apple trees and the garden was a jumble of colour with bright flowers gaily blooming. Tope took me on a guided tour before entering through the front door, which had two tubs of tiger lilies flanking it. So this was where Tope had settled down after she was demobbed.

'I call this my rest house,' she told me as she ran a proud eye over the interior. 'When the sanatorium discharges terminal cases, this is where they come for sanctuary.

Often, even those who are not so seriously ill land up and beg me to take them in. I have to relent in some cases.' She shrugged. 'I charge each one a thousand rupees per season, which includes their board, lodging and laundry as well. And because I charge so little, I have to literally throw some of them out.' She laughed. 'However, I have two rules,' she declared as she wiggled two fat fingers in front of me. 'One: woman patient, absolutely not allowed; and two: pay up before coming in, so that if a patient pops off before the month is over, I am not left in the lurch. However, once in a while, I take some cases in for charity's sake. I have one right now, in fact. Poor chap, he has a first-class-first degree in MSc and was a research scholar when he fell prey to this disease. I told him, "Don't worry, baba, come over. The sanatorium may be a heartless institution, but Tope's heart is large enough for all!"'

How right she was, although Tope's large heart had space only for men. When she introduced me to her lodgers, I was stunned. None of them looked ill, leave alone as if they were dying: they had pink cheeks, well filled-out limbs and were in splendid spirits.

'If only you had seen them last year . . .' she started and then broke off to call out to one of them. 'Hardeep, son, go get that group photo for me.' She pulled me down to the comfortable divan.

Hardeep had a triangular face, slanting eyes and a sharply angled knot on the top of his head. An athlete, he had picked up tuberculosis somewhere along the way. He ran immediately to fetch the album Tope asked for. I saw a photo of them when they had come to her: they looked like four cadavers ready to mount their funeral pyres.

'See, see,' Tope pointed them out with her fat finger, 'Dr Khazan in the sanatorium had given them just four months to live, but I gifted them a new life! And do you know how? Goat's milk, apple juice – and tra-la-la-la,' she sang as she drummed her stomach like a drum. It was true! All four of them looked perfectly healthy now: Hardeep, the marathon man; the dancer Maganlal Chhaganlal Patel, who had entranced the Russians with his lithe body on a cultural tour there; and the squat Radheshyam Maheshwari, whom Tope had nicknamed 'Midget'. But the one who really held my attention was the fourth lodger – Rajinder Singh. He was the quietest and most polite of them and I figured he must be one of her 'charity cases'. All of them leapt and jumped like playful bunnies and helped themselves to the apples she had just brought, fighting over the strawberries that lay hidden at the bottom of the basket.

'Mummy, they've conned you again with sour ones,' piped up Midget, perched on a windowsill. 'How much did you pay for these?' He took another bite from an apple.

'No, Midget, you have nothing to do with the prices,' she admonished him. 'Eat up!' And Midget immediately pouted in mock anger.

'He is a baniya, Mummy,' said Hardeep. 'Yesterday, he wanted to know the price of the goat's milk, don't you remember?' And the divan shook as Tope guffawed. 'O Sardara' – she wiped her eyes – 'you'll be the death of me one day.' She giggled. 'The jokes this boy can tell!' She looked at me, shaking her head. 'You should hear his Sardar jokes, I tell you. No one can tell Sardar jokes better than a Sardar himself!'

Rajinder wiped his thick glasses quietly, not even smiling at this merry exchange. I looked at him: Tope's brilliant research scholar was truly good-looking. Without his glasses, he looked like an innocent schoolboy. Obviously, Tope's unique goat milk and apple juice therapy had worked its wonder on him. However, there was something sad about him.

'He's very shy,' Tope said as if to answer my unspoken question. 'If God wills, one day he will win the Nobel prize for physics . . .'

I spent two lovely days with Tope, charmed by her hospitality and her remarkable hospice. She really cared for her patients and kept her cottage so clean that you could see your face on the tiles of the floor. There was one ayah and two bearers, and when they served food on the table, you really felt pampered. Meals were served with clockwork precision, on the dot of the hour fixed by her. She herself gave out the portions. 'Hardeep, why have you left that egg uneaten on your plate? Midget, you must finish that beetroot, and you, Patel, why are you playing billiards on your plate with the fork and knife?'

Often, Patel would get lost in the memories of past recitals and play around with his food, his mind clearly elsewhere.

'Oh, sorry, Mummy! Very sorry!' he replied and started working his way through a large helping of chicken.

'And you, my angel, are you troubled by memories of your university?' she'd ask Rajinder tenderly. 'This one has to be fed by me,' she told me, pulling her chair close to his.

Tope's quartet came to see me off to the bus stand and, although I invited them all warmly to come to Nainital and stay with me, they never did.

That year, my husband was posted to Agra and, at Christmas, I got a rather sweet card. There was only one person who was likely to send me Christmas greetings, I thought, as I tore open the envelope. I was right: the card, with snowy mountains and a couple on a sledge, was signed, 'With best wishes from Tope and Rajinder'.

Why just Rajinder? What had happened to Hardeep, Midget and Patel? Perhaps they had gone away after getting cured, I shrugged and put the card away. Eight days later, I got a telegram: 'Coming to Agra to see Taj' and the senders were 'Tope and Rajinder'.

I was quite puzzled. Why was Tope coming with Rajinder to see the Taj by moonlight? Perhaps she was fulfilling his last wish to see the Taj in the light of a full moon before he died, I thought. Or maybe they were coming just for a little break from the cold winter in Bhowali. Not only did she look after their meals and medicines, she often took care of their entertainment, sometimes finding girlfriends for her lonely lodgers. Her niece, Padmawati Robert, was a teacher in Bhowali and Tope would ask her to bring along a few young girls when she came to visit her aunt. 'So that my boys have a good time,' she had confided in me. May be this was why she was bringing Rajinder to see the Taj. Whatever the reason, I was so fond of Tope that I decided to go and fetch her from the railway station myself in my car.

When Tope and Rajinder alighted from the train, I gulped at the sight. She brought to mind the old Almora Tope, who flirted shamelessly with the Australian soldiers, lips aglow with scarlet lipstick. I am certain some of them remembered her to their dying day. Here she was, scarlet lipstick, bright red sari to match, costume jewellery on her ears and neck. And with her was Rajinder, with his sad eyes and serious face.

Tope waved cheerily when she saw me and anointed both my cheeks with loud, smacking kisses. 'We decided to inaugurate our honeymoon with a trip to Shah Jahan's monument of love, isn't it darling?' she said and pressed Rajinder's hand.

I was speechless. What on earth had possessed a handsome young man to marry this old, painted tart? I thought of my conservative family and thanked god silently for sending my husband on a tour to Delhi. But how would I explain her to the children? I had grown-up daughters, and what would they say when they saw this friend of Mummy's?

As soon as they could, my daughters pulled me aside. 'Chhi, Mummy, even the servants are laughing at them! He could put Rock Hudson to shame – but your friend! Who does she think she is?'

I couldn't tell them that twenty-five years ago, Tope had considered herself no less than Ginger Rogers, and even today, she thinks she is better-looking than Liz Taylor. Perhaps my bhabhi had a point when she said that Tope carried colour inside her. Each day, she changed into loud clothes – shocking pink, lurid green and electric blue – as she and her husband went shopping and sightseeing. I had taken great care to give them the best time I could, but come mealtimes, Tope would revert to her stern Mummy self. 'No, darling, no samosa for you,' she'd say and take it out of Rajinder's hands. 'You know that fried food is bad for you, it makes your tummy run, remember? And must you have tea? Drink milk instead. Tea does not suit your digestion.' When I saw her behave like this, I wondered why this promising young man had surrendered so tamely to Tope. For three days, she dragged him around Agra and allowed him nothing more than fruit and milk. By the fourth day, he looked as if he'd drop dead. I bade them a relieved goodbye and after one letter of thanks to me, Tope went silent all over again.

Next year, I was returning after a wedding in the family and had to spend one night in the Retiring Room in Lucknow's railway station. 'There's a terrible rush,' said the station master when I went to see him about a room. 'There is just one spare bed in a double room, if you don't mind sharing it with another lady passenger.'

I was so exhausted that I said I didn't care who it was. Like most cavernous waiting rooms in colonial buildings, this one was large and airy, but so ill-lit that I could not make out who was lying in the other bed. Anyway, that person had pulled the sheet over her head and looked like a beached whale. Or like a corpse in a mortuary, waiting for a post-mortem. Suppose it was a man, I thought, this person looked like no woman and had no familiar curves, except a huge belly. I was still wondering whether I should stay or spend the night sitting in the Waiting Room downstairs when a passing train shrieked loudly. The sleeping giant got up with a start, and when she pulled the sheet off her head, I realized that this was not some unknown man but my old friend Tope!

'Oh my God! Oh Jesus! Praise the Lord! I wondered whether I'd ever see you again, and look what He sent me today!' she greeted me effusively.

'Are you all right, Tope?' I asked. 'You're not looking at all well.' Without her make-up on, she looked terribly old and pasty.

'I am fine,' she replied. 'Just tired and stressed, darling. You see, I've just come back from Haridwar,' she told me.

Now, I knew that Tope was a devout Christian, that she went to church every Sunday and kissed the Bible dozens of times in a day, so what on earth was she doing in Haridwar?

'I went to immerse Rajinder's ashes,' she explained. Then she sighed deeply. 'What could I write and tell you? He'd become so stubborn and disobedient of late. He just wouldn't listen to me any more. Gave up drinking goat's milk and apple juice and went crazy about films – began to watch three or four in a day! I told him to see decent Hollywood films,' she said angrily, 'but he would have none of it. It was the cheap excitement of those Hindi films that was his undoing.' She shook her head sadly.

So he did revolt, I thought to myself.

'He was ill for just two days, and then poof!' She snapped her fingers. 'Hardeep, Midget, Patel – all of them listened to me, and so even though their lungs had turned to sawdust by the time they came to me, they survived.'

Both of us were silent. After a while, she spoke again: 'All Rajinder had said to me before dying was that I should immerse his ashes in Haridwar. After he died, I first thought of getting a nice marble gravestone made for him, but I know that his soul would have escaped from there and run to Haridwar.'

She choked and took off her glasses to wipe her tears. She had put her dentures on the bedside table and, suddenly, Tope looked old and defeated.

My heart melted. 'Come with me, Tope,' I said impulsively. 'Stay a few days with me. The children will cheer you up.'

'Thank you, darling,' she said. 'But I am not alone, you know. Jesus keeps sending me sick people to look after. I've just taken on another charity case: lovely boy! Samuel is in his last year of medical school. He's got pleurisy, so he's taken a year off. If God wills, he will get the Nobel prize for medicine one day. I have to get back to him. We'll meet again, honey,' she said as she collected her stuff. 'Never fear!' And with a familiar flying kiss, she left to catch her train.

After that meeting, I dreaded every day I spent in Agra in case she arrived with a new husband for another honeymoon. Then, one Christmas, a card arrived: two lovebirds on a telegraph pole, their beaks kissing each other. The senders were 'Tope and Samuel'.

Clearly, Tope had found another husband to replace the one she had lost. And this time, when he died, she would be free to bury him under a marble gravestone. This one would not escape to Haridwar, I knew. Not if Tope had her way. And when he died, her beloved Jesus would send her another one. Tope knew that He would make sure that she was never left alone.

The Life and Literature of Shivani

P.S.

Insights
Interviews &
More . . .

Shivani

b. 17 October 1923
d. 21 March 2003

Shivani was born in Rajkot, Gujarat, and went to Santiniketan in 1935, at the age of twelve, and was there for nine years, graduating from Calcutta University in 1944.

She was awarded the Padma Shri in 1983. She was also a recipient of the Bhartendu Harishchandra Puraskar (Hindi Urdu Academy, Lucknow), Premchand Puraskar, Bankim Puraskar (Kolkata), Maharashtra Rajya Hindi Akademy Samman, Kendriya Hindi Sansthan (Agra) and Uttar Pradesh Hindi Sansthan Puraskar. Kanpur University presented her with an honorary doctorate in 1994.

Shivani published her first short story 'Lal Haveli' in *Dharmayug* in 1958. Her first novel *Mayapuri* was published in 1961.

Published Works

The Life and Literature of Shivani

Mrinal Pande

All books published by Radhakrishna Prakashan, Daryaganj, New Delhi

As years go, the year 1971 came close to being an *annus horribilis* for Shivani. Her husband, our father, was terminally ill. Her youngest daughter Ira, the translator of these stories, was about to be married. Two other daughters were far away and burdened with infants and her only son, fresh out of school, was just about settling down to the exacting schedule of an IIT.

Most would have collapsed under the burden of a host of necessary and unnecessary arrangements and the constant and chaotic comings and goings of doctors, caterers, priests and tailors all through the day. But even as she paid some, bargained and quarrelled with

Novels

Mayapuri

Chaudah Phere

Krishnakali

Bhairavi

Vishkanya

Smashan Champa

others and turned some away, Shivani found time to write. Late at night, early in the morning, she quietly put together the pieces that went on to make a memorable work *Apradhini* ('The Sinners'). Published in 1972 as a collection of interviews, this was perhaps the first book of its kind, in which a popular Hindi writer had tried painstakingly to profile the lives of indigent women behind bars. To these, Ira and I have taken the liberty to append a few more of her sketches of ordinary women with extraordinary lives.

The women the reader encounters here are ordinary beings without access to money, knowledge, any familial or outside support. And yet, they are all trying hard to hold on to their lives and dignity in a society which has traditionally been less than kind to women and positively hostile to women without men. Compared to the simple, basic needs they articulate, the needs of their fellow men sound aggressive, stupid or farfetched. Once they are out, the women say that they only need to be mobile without fear, to communicate with their loved ones, to touch their children once again, to sit under the trees in their own courtyards and feel the sun warm their tired bones. Grey, tired and anxious as many of them are, within the prison all their instincts are focused on surviving their term. Their stories are different, for each bears a separate cross. Yet, beneath the vivid details of their lives, is a common knowledge, a single pain: each of them is doomed to suffer alone.

Shivani's dislike for analysing or judging these women is due not to an obstinacy but because of a deep knowledge about the nasty, brutish and heavily exploited lives of women without men. They have been beaten, cheated and bullied by men all their lives, but like addicts craving a fix, most of them turn to men again and again, making the same mistake twice, thrice, a hundred times. Shivani is here the witness and fellow traveller become historian.

*

He who gathers knowledge gathers pain, the Bible says. And Shivani had gathered much pain during her long life. She knew that to record pain, it is necessary first to make a supreme effort of will to detach the mind completely from the ordinary affairs of everyday life. Difficult enough for a man, this effort is near impossible for a woman from a traditional family, burdened with multiple responsibilities as a mother and wife.

Novels

Kainja

Rati Vilap

Surangama

Novels

Kishnuli

Krishna Veni

Chal Khusro Ghar Aapney

Even as she sat recording these intricate real-life stories of women criminals, scoundrels, thieves, murderers, whores and sanyasins, Shivani knew she herself could not afford to shake off her own worldly duties as wife, mother and daughter with a grand gesture, like most of her male counterparts. She was expected to observe proprieties, keep the family name intact and, at the same time, also shoulder the burden of the family that neither her bedridden husband nor her children could handle at that point. Already her itinerant travels and hugely popular stories about men and women and their lusts and longings were drawing much adverse comments from the hidebound Kumaoni Brahmin community that she belonged to and had married her daughters into. She could not afford to ruffle more feathers at this point. The house had to be run, college fees had to be provided for and marriage preparations had to be made. So she wrote and got up frequently to do what needed to be done and, knitting together those thick eyebrows in a deep frown, came back and wrote some more. She did not complain. Who could she have complained to, anyhow?

Siddhartha became the Buddha, one reads, after leaving his family behind and wandering all over in search of Truth. Having found Bodhi Gyan, he declared that the world was merely a mirage, Maya. Legend also has it that after following Alexander on his long historic voyage to Asia, Pyrrhon, the painter, too gave up painting and became the founder of Scepticism, a philosophy that declared the whole world to be an illusion. As she wrote, Shivani too came to the same conclusion. She wraps up her introduction to the book with the haunting lines sung by three fakirs in a play:

Gul shor babula aag hava
aur keechad pani mitti hai
Hum dekh chuke is duniya ko
Yeh dhokhey ki ik tatti hai

A ball of fire, a gust of hot wind
Mud, water and slime
We have seen this world, my friends
It is nothing but a mirage . . .

*

Shivani's presence as a visiting writer in the Lucknow prison was made possible by the overwhelming kindness of a fan: a doctor who attended on these incarcerated women. So these visits owed nothing to any institution or authority.

Novels

Vivart

Kalindi

Atithi

Pootonvalee

Short Stories

Kariye Chhima

Pushphaar

Lal Haveli

Here, in these stories, Shivani sits among women prisoners merely as a humble witness to human pain. When these women weep in her lap, touch her feet and drink the water that has washed her hands, calling it 'gangajal', they are not posturing – nor is she exaggerating. They are convinced that they weep in a lap that has been enriched by experience and is forgiving of all sins. To protect her already somewhat besmirched reputation for fraternizing below her social class, Shivani could perhaps have resorted to the traditional trick of writing: get a fabricated narrator to present a carefully doctored version of reality.

But she chose not to.

The stories in this volume are remarkable in that whatever is said here is validated by the fact that the writer has been there herself, both as a witness and storyteller. To some, a certain egoism may seem to be lurking in this technique, specially at places where the writer complains about the relentless heat and filth of a prison or the personal humiliations and the boredom she had to suffer in the company of petty snobs or nasty and judgmental women. Yet, it was important to Shivani that the stories be authenticated by what she as witness was herself undergoing as she collected and recorded these remarkable stories.

*

Shivani grew up in an age when families who curbed the natural high spirits of gifted children with an iron hand were merely called strict and sensible. Girls and women were expected to keep their gaze lowered and their mouths shut until asked to speak up. And timidity and demure deference were deemed virtues to be cultivated by all good and homely girls.

'She was a tough filly, your mother,' our grandmother, Ama, told us again and again. 'She needed a tough malik like your father to break her.' Ama also told us how worried it had made her to know that as a young student in Santiniketan, her spirited and high-strung daughter had suddenly taken to the dangerous habit of walking in her sleep. There was no curbing her, she said again and again, shaking her head in sorrow.

My mother's explanation was simple: 'I heard someone call me in my dream and I suppose I just got up and went. I had no idea who it was or why. I only remember my roommates telling me the next day that I had caused a big

Short Stories

Meri Priya Kahaniyan

Char Din Ki Chandni

Swayamsiddha

commotion at night when I went missing and was found walking on the parapet of the roof, fast asleep. They had to hold their breath till I walked down and came back to my room and went to sleep in my bed. I remembered nothing of all this. My friends took to sleeping next to me and we'd tie our pigtails together when we went to sleep so that, in case I tried to get out again, we'd both be jolted awake.'

Did it work?

'I don't remember, but it stopped after a while, so I forgot all about it.'

This nonchalance was typical of her. When asked how she, with her firebrand reputation, had agreed to marry a widower she had never met and who was, moreover, ten years her senior, her reply was simple and matter of fact. 'I had no father and Ija (her mother) was worried. How could I say no and let her down?'

She gave up walking in her sleep, but her nightmares continued till the end of her life. We were often jolted awake by a strange howl emanating from her bedroom in the dead of the night. It was the howl of a wounded animal, inhuman and disembodied, and it froze the marrow in our bones every time. We'd gently coax her awake and she'd be deeply remorseful the next morning. But then life resumed its predictable course.

Could it be that her spirit craved a freedom denied her in her real life?

Could it be that over and above that which she recorded, there was a lot that she had seen and experienced which remained unsaid and, in the dead of the night, it was this that was crying out to be released?

We will never know.

*

We will also never know for sure if, in profiling the complex lives and minds of the women criminals and sanyasins who stand outside the pale of traditional Hindu society, Shivani is also looking at herself, her own life. But what we do see is that her composure as the narrator in these stories coexists with a deep personal hurt. Because as a fatherless girl and later as a widow, she had been judged so often without being given a chance to explain herself, Shivani understood the unspoken anxieties of women without men. She listened and recorded their tales whenever she could. She knew how society mostly chose to ignore women's own experiences and how families could be exclusively obsessed with the social propriety of the actions and speech of women alone. So she

Kasturee Mrig

Chir Swayamvara

Shivani Ki Sreshtha Kahaniyan

turns again and again to redeem for posterity the unmentionable truth of experiences misjudged, disinherited and lonely women of all ages have had.

Personally, Shivani abhorred social dos such as weddings and sacred thread ceremonies, which showcased women as men's prized possessions. The usual talk on such occasions about expenses and the crass display of superiority in the observance of simple rituals moved and depressed her. She felt that those who were excited about them were like children, afraid of defying little understood and moribund traditions but ashamed to confess so. When she had to attend social functions for duty's sake, she'd arrive wrapped in a certain queenly aloofness. She was perceptive, quick-witted and rudely dismissive of bores. And till the end of her days, remained a somewhat intimidating presence at all traditional social get-togethers. Most people hesitated before they spoke to her, others declared her too proud and arrogant for a widow with no great income. The truth was that they were afraid of her sharp powers of observation and of being presented as a character in her stories, warts and all. Shivani was proud, but she was not arrogant: she just refused to suffer fools gladly or smile when she felt no need to. The power of her intimidating presence was of a kind that belongs to a sanyasin who has voluntarily given up all earthly trappings of power and, with that, also the desire to judge. Of course, she tried hard to play the meek lamb – but it was hard to hide her regal stripes.

The female body and its yearnings that startle us in *Apradhini* are central to many of Shivani's writings. Although she was brought up like most Hindu upper-caste women to believe that the worth of a female body lies in the male gaze, she could see that this was not entirely true, nor right. All around her she could see men, even the good-for-nothing, feeble-bodied ones, firmly in control of women's bodies. Their women were their ultimate trophies to play around with, display or destroy. To discover and highlight how some women fought against the given situation while others went under and never resurfaced, Shivani liked to focus on women who lived in isolation, self-imposed or forced. In *Apradhini,* prison and the robes of a nomadic female sanyasin are the petri dishes upon which Shivani lays her specimens and studies relentlessly how women may survive without men, often in spite of them. The exercise is rooted

Uppreti

Manimala Ki Hansi

in the timeless quest of artists to uncover the secret of the irreverent, timeless vitality of certain exiled species, who continue under the most adverse circumstances and even outlive mighty empires. If fashion and medicine give the female body a centrality, prisons make them invisible and sanyas makes them irrelevant. Dressed in coarse prison garments, all women prisoners begin to look alike after a while. And the saffron robes of an itinerant sanyasin like Alakh Mai efface gender completely.

The sanyasins and prosperous whores who appear here and generally all over Shivani's writings are important to her. They are answerable only to themselves and are free and mobile in a way most women can only dream of being. Later, Shivani talks in her autobiography about a strange visit to the temple of Kali in a forest near Santiniketan, which frightened and also charged her with a strange energy, just as Alakh Mai's touch had done years ago. Kali was a goddess she grew up with and also what a high-caste Hindu girl like her associated pure sexuality and/or androgynous intellect with. She, who is the patron goddess of all the groups and individuals who defy the near-total ban on the mobility and taboos of carefree fraternizing between women and men, has driven the energies of many Indian writers, from Kalidasa to Banbhatt. Kali's power over words, her wild abandon to love and lust and her astounding mobility makes her specially attractive to all seekers of Truth, from Alakh Mai to Shivani. The lives of characters like Madhu Ben, Alakh Mai and Rajula may be full of hardships and penance, but the act of walking through a wilderness, preferably alone, is also what true pilgrimages of self-discovery are made of.

It was for this reason that Shivani turned again and again to the world of social pariahs, even naturally cagey criminals and deviants of all kinds. They may be traitors to social norms, but to her they are brave human beings who had the courage to be truthful to themselves in the face of great odds. The pariahs, in turn, were not just automatically drawn to her but also trusted her. They saw in her an honest listener and recorder of their innermost feelings and hidden desires. Ironically, it was for this reason that her own relatives were so often ashamed of her. They loved her, but they also wanted her silent and obedient like other women of her age. They suffered with every word she wrote and rejoiced at every story she

Memoirs and Essays

Manjeer

Kyon

Jaalak

Smriti Kalash

Memoirs and Essays

Vatayan

Ek Thi Ramrati

Mera Bhai

Shivani Ke Sreshtha Rekha Chitra

didn't write. They were such brave relatives, ready to humiliate one of the rarest talents in their midst for the sake of a tradition that made slaves out of women.

When Shivani created a rare portrait gallery of women without men, she did not seek to avenge her own humiliations. She only wished to highlight women who were different. Like herself. The strange wandering women she met and befriended from Almora to Gujarat, or the female prisoners she talked to as a young girl in Rampur and Orchha and later in Lucknow, are neither good nor bad. They are just some of the millions of rudderless individuals who subsist in the moral and physical decay of Indian society. They are not alienated from society – many of them, like her own mother, are in touch socially or emotionally and even rationally – they understand the social mores and have tried to follow them. It is just that, like the writer they are talking to, they cannot frequently make sense of the laws they are supposed to obey nor the punishments they have been given.

As the stories unfold, we begin to see that there is an irony in Shivani's portrayal of women that pierces the mind and reminds us of a certain spiritual nakedness we all share with these dispossessed souls. They talk and she listens keenly in a space unguarded, unsupervised and unedited by a male presence. Rereading the stories after a gap of several years, I realize that, precarious and ambiguous as several of these tales are, they point at a reality far beyond what mere words can record.

*

Yatrik Charaiveti

Mobility, that mother of all freedoms, is something that did not come to young women in Shivani's time as easily and as matter of course as it did to young men. Even to women from privileged families studying at Santiniketan. And freedom was what young Gaura, who was yet to become Shivani, or our mother, craved. She, who was born under the star of Venus, was yet to awaken to her gifts of creativity, but her heart knew as certainly as a bird's does what the utter abandonment of a long, unhindered flight must feel like. We only know from her early pictures what a strong, tough traveller our mother was as a young student. There she is, scowling or squinting in the sun, carrying a gigantic holdall slung on a pole with her mates, sitting astride a bullock cart sucking on

Bachpan Ki Yaad

Radhika Sundari

Harhar Gangey

a stick of sugarcane, sitting in a boat watching the French film-maker Renoir shoot his series on the Ganga, riding a horse in jodhpurs. My own earliest memories of her are of her beautiful tall frame in a simple *tangail* sari, her head demurely draped as a mark of respect for my father's father, gazing out as the sun set over the hills.

I can see how after getting married into a traditional family soon after her graduation Shivani must have tried hard to toe the line all married women in her husband's family were expected to. This phase did not last too long: it could not. Female relatives ribbed her mercilessly later, in our presence, about how she quickly gave up covering her head once her father-in-law died and how she lacked feminine graces despite her high education. They pointed out how she lacked the basic skills in housekeeping and how the straps of her bra and the hem of her petticoats were always showing from beneath her garments. I also remember, when I returned long after my father's death, various relatives sniggering or erupting angrily as they told me how nothing – but nothing – had prevented our mother from writing and reading in that hour of family crisis. About how she'd casually wear red even after her husband had been cremated; about how she, a widow, would think nothing of going and reading her stories on the radio before the mandatory first year of mourning for her husband was over.

As a person, Shivani was hurt but not diminished by such attitudes. True, she was always restless and unpredictable. This was unusual in a country where women, as mothers and wives, are expected to be the gentle and stable half in any marriage. It was also true that sometimes her artistic instincts took precedence over her family ones. This trait did not so much irritate as puzzle me. Things fell in place when I read Darwin's *The Descent of Man*. There, he notes how the migratory impulses in certain birds may prove to be stronger than their maternal ones and, when the time comes, such a bird mother may even leave her fledglings behind to follow the flock on its long journey. He quotes the example of Audubon's goose, which, when deprived of feathers, set out on her journey on foot. He also describes the pain and horror of a bird, caged forcibly at the time of its annual migratory journey, and how it bloodied its breast trying to break the restrictive bars of its cage.

Books for Children

Alvida

Bhoot Uncle

Ice-cream Mahal

As she sat writing out these pieces on the dining table late into the night at 66 Gulistan Colony, perhaps my mother too was answering some mysterious call of her creative mind and purging her own demons at the same time. And this was what kept her going.

'Write, Shivani, write' – all her fellow artists, travellers in the same boat, from Mahadevi Verma and Begum Akhtar to Amritlal Nagar and Shankho Da, had advised her when my father died.

Shivani wrote and thus survived as Scheherazade had done before her, and Meera and Mahadevi.

'Shivani' was the pseudonym of writer Gaura Pant (1923–2003). She attained cult status in the Hindi literary world in the 1960s and 1970s and was awarded the Padma Shri in 1983. Her best-known works include the novels *Chaudah Phere*, *Krishnakali*, *Smashan Champa*, *Rati Vilap* and *Vishkanya*.

Ira Pande is a writer and translator. She has translated several books from Hindi into English. She recieved the Vodafone Crossword Book Award and the Sahitya Akademi Translation Prize for her translation of Manohar Shyam Joshi's *T'ta Professor* in 2009 and 2010 respectively.

HARPERPERENNIAL

Harper Perennial presents special editions of
its finest books in translation

Apradhini
Shivani
Translated from the Hindi by Ira Pande

Avasthe
U.R. Ananthamurthy
Translated from the Kannada by Narayan Hegde

Blue Is Like Blue
Vinod Kumar Shukla
Translated from the Hindi by Arvind Krishna Mehrotra and Sara Rai

Diary of a Malayali Madman
N. Prabhakaran
Translated from the Malayalam by Jayasree Kalathil

Farewell, Mahatma
Devibharathi
Translated from the Tamil by N. Kalyan Raman

The Golden Gandhi Statue from America
Subimal Misra
Translated from the Bengali by V. Ramaswamy

A Name for Every Leaf
Ashok Vajpeyi
Translated from the Hindi by Rahul Soni

Moustache
S. Hareesh
Translated from the Malayalam by Jayasree Kalathil

Seven Sixes Are Forty-Three
Kiran Nagarkar
Translated from the Marathi by Shubha Slee

Shameless
Taslima Nasreen
Translated from the Bengali by Arunava Sinha

HARPERPERENNIAL

Age of Frenzy
Mahabaleshwar Sail
Translated from the Konkani by Vidya Pai

A Life Incomplete
Nanak Singh
Translated from the Punjabi by Navdeep Suri

Mohanaswamy
Vasudhendra
Translated from the Kannada by Rashmi Terdal

The Music of Solitude
Krishna Sobti
Translated from the Hindi by Vasudha Dalmia

No Presents Please
Jayant Kaikini
Translated from the Kannada by Tejaswini Niranjana

A Preface to Man
Subhash Chandran
Translated from the Malayalam by Fathima E.V.

The Secret Garland
Andal
Translated from the Tamil by Archana Venkatesan

Shala
Milind Bokil
Translated from the Marathi by Vikrant Pande

The Weary Generations
Abdullah Hussein
Translated from the Urdu by the author

Written in Tears
Arupa Patangia Kalita
Translated from the Assamese by Ranjita Biswas

HARPERPERENNIAL

Bhima
M.T. Vasudevan Nair
Translated from the Malayalam by Gita Krishnankutty

Chemmeen
Thakazhi Sivasankara Pillai
Translated from the Malayalam by Anita Nair

Ghachar Ghochar
Vivek Shanbhag
Translated from the Kannada by Srinath Perur

Hindutva or Hind Swaraj
U.R. Ananthamurthy
Translated from the Kannada by Keerti Ramachandra and Vivek Shanbhag

The Liberation of Sita
Volga
Translated from the Telugu by T. Vijay Kumar and C. Vijayasree

A Life Misspent
Suryakant Tripathi Nirala
Translated from the Hindi by Satti Khanna

The Sea Lies Ahead
Intizar Husain
Translated from the Urdu by Rakhshanda Jalil

Selected Poems
Joy Goswami
Translated from the Bengali by Sampurna Chattarji

Wild Animals Prohibited
Subimal Misra
Translated from the Bengali by V. Ramaswamy

Wild Words
Malathi Maithri, Salma, Kutti Revathi and Sukirtharani
Translated from the Tamil by Lakshmi Holmström

HarperCollins *Publishers* India

At HarperCollins India, we believe in telling the best stories and finding the widest readership for our books in every format possible. We started publishing in 1992; a great deal has changed since then, but what has remained constant is the passion with which our authors write their books, the love with which readers receive them, and the sheer joy and excitement that we as publishers feel in being a part of the publishing process.

Over the years, we've had the pleasure of publishing some of the finest writing from the subcontinent and around the world, including several award-winning titles and some of the biggest bestsellers in India's publishing history. But nothing has meant more to us than the fact that millions of people have read the books we published, and that somewhere, a book of ours might have made a difference.

As we look to the future, we go back to that one word—a word which has been a driving force for us all these years.

Read.